# EASY NIGHTS

## A BOUDREAUX NOVEL

## KRISTEN PROBY

AMPERSAND PUBLISHING, INC.

Easy Nights
Book Six in the Boudreaux Series
By
Kristen Proby

EASY NIGHTS

Book Six in The Boudreaux Series

Kristen Proby

Copyright © 2017 by Kristen Proby

Cover Design: Okay Creations

Published by Ampersand Publishing, Inc.

Paperback ISBN: 978-1-63350-093-8

This one is for John.
You are the greatest light in my life, and
the best part of every day.
I love you.

*ifteen Years Ago...*

"You cut your hair," Ben says as he comes into the dining room. He stops short when he sees me, a frown covering his handsome face.

*He noticed!*

I weave my fingertips through my dark brown hair and give him a tentative smile. "Just yesterday."

"Why?"

I frown at his harsh tone.

"Because I wanted to."

He sits next to me, like he does every Tuesday and Thursday afternoon, and I can't help but take a deep breath, absorbing his smell.

Ben always smells amazing. Like sunshine and hard work and... *sexy.*

"Van?" he says, getting my attention.

"I'm sorry, what?"

1

He shakes his head, a smile tickling his lips now. "You're such a daydreamer."

*Only when you're around.*

I would never blatantly say anything like that. Flirting with my older brother's best friend isn't the smart thing to do. Eli and Beau might make Ben stay away from me, and that just can't happen.

*I love him so much it hurts.*

"What do you think of my hair?"

He shrugs one shoulder and grabs my math textbook, opening to the chapter we're currently working on. I am *horrific* at math, but Ben is a genius at it, and he's been helping me with my math homework for the past three months.

It's heaven.

"It's fine."

"You don't like it."

He shrugs again. "I liked it long."

For half a second, I regret chopping it off, taking it from almost reaching my butt to just barely reaching my shoulders.

It's so much lighter!

But then I let it roll off of me because *I* do like it. I have to live with it. No man is ever going to tell me how I should wear my hair. This isn't the dark ages.

"Did you do your homework from last night?" he asks, and I nod, handing him my notebook so he can look over my work.

I've never loved math so much in my life.

He's biting the inside of his cheek as he looks over my paper and when he's finished, he turns those blue eyes to me with a smile. "You're picking it up really well. You won't even need me once I leave next month."

And just like that, my happy mood crumbles like a sandcastle under the tide.

Ben's leaving. He's going away to college, and the closer the time comes, the more panicked I am. I don't want him to go.

Ben nudges me with his elbow.

"I'll still need you," I mumble, not able to look him in the eyes because I'm afraid that he'll see right through me, and he'll be repulsed at the idea of his best friend's little sister having the hots for him.

Or, far worse, he'll feel sorry for me, and the thought of that makes me want to throw up.

"I'll check in on you when I'm home on my breaks," he says and sets my notebook in front of me as he turns to this week's chapter.

For the next two hours, he walks me through the steps that the teacher showed us in class, but Ben's voice is so much easier to listen to, and he explains things thoroughly, making sure I understand before we move on.

He's an excellent teacher. In fact, he's going to college to be a teacher. He will rock it.

I just wish he didn't have to go so far away to college. Beau's been there for a year already, and Eli and Ben are going to the same one, and they're all going to rent an apartment together.

I frown and try not to think about all of the college girls that will be around, hitting on Ben. Will he sleep with them? Date them?

Eventually marry one of them?

Jesus, I hope not.

"Why can't you focus today?" Ben finally asks, bringing my attention back to the here and now.

"Sorry," I whisper.

"What's wrong, Vanny?"

I roll my eyes. "I hate it when you call me that."

His lips twitch in humor. "I know. Talk to me. What's wrong?"

"Maybe I just didn't get enough sleep last night." It's not a lie; I didn't sleep well last night.

"Hmm." He studies me closely for a second. "You look well rested."

"I'm fine."

He tilts his head to the side. "Don't ever lie to me, Savannah."

His eyes are narrowed, and between that hot look and his firm voice, well, I guess you'd say I'm all kinds of turned on.

So of course Eli pokes his head around the corner, interrupting us.

"Ben, are you going to come shoot hoops with us?"

"Yeah, we're almost done here."

Eli nods and disappears, and I want to beg Ben not to go. Don't go shoot hoops, don't go away to college.

Stay with me.

But that's dumb, and he'd probably laugh at me and tell me I'm being stupid. I'm just a kid, after all. Fifteen-year-olds don't have anything figured out, and I'm a baby.

But I don't feel like a baby when he's near. Not at all.

Ben cocks a brow, waiting for me to answer him.

"I'm not lying." I shrug a shoulder and do my best to look like I've got all of my feelings under control.

I should win an Oscar for this performance.

"You've got this handled," Ben says with a smile after studying me for a moment. "You're doing great, Van. I'm going to go shoot with the guys, but I'll be around later if you have any questions."

"Okay." I smile and nod, turning my attention to my homework. "Thanks."

"Van?"

My head whips up. "Yeah?"

"Even though I like your hair longer, this is cute too."

He grins and winks at me, and then he's gone, and I'm left sitting here in the dining room, my hands sweaty, and a stupid grin on my face.

Ben thinks my hair is cute.

It's a start.

## CHAPTER 1

~SAVANNAH~

*P*resent Day
Two years.

It's been two years since the day I thought I was going to die, but instead I was set free.

I didn't sleep last night, but that's not new. I haven't been able to sleep well in years. It's probably the biggest thing that I still carry with me from my marriage, and no matter what I do, I can't seem to change it.

But compared to where I was two years ago, not sleeping great is not worth complaining about.

I stare at myself in my vanity mirror, my brush clenched in my white knuckles and search my unblemished face. I can still see the bruises from that last beating. The marks around my neck from where he savagely strangled me. The wet hair from the tub where he tried to drown me. I can still feel the humiliation when my siblings came running into the bedroom after I called them for help.

Even Ben came, and that was the biggest humiliation of all. I never wanted *anyone* to ever see me like that, especially the man that I've loved my entire adult life. For a moment, I'd almost wished that Lance had done the job of killing me, just so I wouldn't have to see the absolute fury and disgust in Ben's face.

These two years have gone by in the blink of an eye, and yet, there were moments when I thought the days moved like a glacier. I spent many months living with family, afraid to be alone. I've been through hundreds of hours of therapy, and I take a self defense class every week.

I grin at myself in the mirror.

I'm here, I'm alive, and I don't look like I'm going to break at any moment.

My cheeks have color, my hazel eyes look happy, and my lips curve up in genuine smiles again.

Thank God.

My mom and most of my siblings have already sent me texts this morning, sending words of love and encouragement. Just as I raise the brush to my hair my phone beeps again.

It's my twin brother, Declan.

*I love you.*

I grin, not willing to let any tears fall today, whether they're from sadness or happiness, and reply.

*Love you more.*

I wouldn't have made it through the months after the *incident* without my family. That's not me being dramatic, it's simple honesty.

Without them, I would have lost my mind.

My phone pings again and lights up, catching my eye. But this time, it's not a sibling.

It's Ben.

"And cue the freaking butterflies," I whisper as I check the message.

*Lunch?*

I take a deep breath, close my eyes, and grin. Ben's a man of few words, especially when it comes to the telephone. He's really much better in person.

Except, when I'm with him, I'm the one who ends up being tongue-tied. Holy Jesus, the man has had the same effect on me since I hit puberty.

All rational thought is gone, and all I want to do is climb him like the big oak trees out at my sister's inn.

Ben has been best friends with my brothers since they were young boys, so he was *always* at my house, and I would come up with any reason I could think of to be where he was.

Much to my brothers' dismay.

But then he went off to college, and our lives didn't cross much for a few years. I eventually went to college myself, in Tennessee, and met Lance there.

I frown at myself in the mirror.

"Don't even *think* that asshole's name."

I punch out a quick response to Ben and grin when he immediately replies.

*Usual place, 1:00.*

*Yes, sir.* I laugh as I close out the text and wander into my closet to choose my outfit for today. I decided to take the day away from the office. A woman doesn't escape from the worst horror of her life every day. It should be celebrated.

The alternative is to overthink and get broody, and I've done that way too much over the past two years.

I deliberately select something that *he* would have never let me wear. A pretty pair of blue cropped pants with a white, sleeveless button down top and red ballet flats. *He* would have said that I was showing too much skin. Even in the hottest summer months I wasn't allowed to wear sleeveless tops, or skirts shorter than my ankles. It's wonderful to have a large wardrobe full of pretty things that I love. I reach for my red Louis Vuitton handbag to match my outfit and finish pulling myself together for the day.

And then my phone rings. It's Larry, my ex-husband's brother. Despite the bullshit his brother put me through, Larry has maintained a relationship with me. He was always kind, and I'm glad to still have him in my life. My family was hesitant at first, but Larry has always been respectful, only being around as much as we're all comfortable with. How he was raised in the same house with his brother and didn't turn out completely evil is beyond me.

"Hello?"

"Hey there, hot stuff," he says, making me laugh. "How are you today?"

"Never been better," I reply and grin as I realize that it's not an exaggeration.

"You sound great." I can hear the smile in his voice. "Is it weird that I thought I should check in on you today?"

"Not at all; all of the other important people in my life have done the same. I figured everyone would forget."

He's quiet for a moment. "No one will ever forget, Van. If I had known—"

"We've been over this a thousand times, Larry. It wasn't your fault."

"Right. You're right."

"I know. Thanks for checking in. I really am doing great."

"I'm glad. If you need anything, you know how to find me."

"That I do. Thanks again."

We end the call, and I sit on the ottoman in my closet and just look around the space. I bought this place about a year and a half ago. I never went back to the house that Lance and I owned together. Instead, my family was happy to have me stay with them until I found this house.

Declan and I have enjoyed renovating it, making it exactly right for me.

I check the time and realize that I'm running late, so I grab a pair of sunglasses, my handbag, and keys, and hurry out to my car.

Even my car is new. *He* wouldn't ever let me get the car I wanted because he said it was too much money, that I didn't deserve a luxury car.

Which is just ludicrous. I work my ass off, and my family is worth billions. I can have any car I fucking want. So, one of the first things I did after the divorce was trade in my sensible Ford for the pretty Mercedes convertible I drive now. It's red and has all the bells and whistles.

Just one more way to flip off my shitty past.

It's a beautiful spring day in New Orleans. The trees are blooming, there's a breeze in the air, and birds sing as I drive toward the French Quarter with the top of my car down.

Despite my best efforts, I still arrive ten minutes late, and all of my sisters and sisters-in-law are already at the restaurant.

"I'm sorry," I say, taking my seat. "I was moving slow this morning."

"As you should," Kate says with a smile. "Eli sends his love."

"He texted," I reply. Kate is married to my older brother, Eli. They recently welcomed a beautiful baby girl named Coraline to our family.

In fact, our family has gone from big to huge in the past two years. It seems that once Eli met Kate, each of my siblings found loves of their own, right after each other. I couldn't be happier for all of them.

"I'm being spoiled today," I announce. "I'm having brunch with all of you beauties, and then I'm having lunch with Ben."

"Really," Gabby, the youngest Boudreaux sister, says with a smile. "As in a date?"

"As in lunch," I reply and roll my eyes. "You know as well as I do that Ben is off limits."

"Why is that again?" Callie, Declan's wife, asks.

"She's delusional and thinks that Ben is like a brother to her," Charly says.

"He is," I insist, frowning.

"No, he's not," Gabby replies. "He may be like a brother to Charly and me, but you never thought of him that way."

"I think *you're* the delusional one. Ben and I are good friends, and that's it." My argument sounds weak to my own ears. But that doesn't make it less true.

"Right," Mallory, my oldest brother, Beau's wife says. "So that's why you blush at the mention of his name and bite your lip?"

"Mallory is psychic," Callie says excitedly. "She can tell you if you're supposed to be with Ben."

"No." My voice is firm as I stare each of them down. "Stop it. Ben is my friend, and I'm not going to fuck that up. If we tried to have a relationship and it didn't work out, he'd be out of my life completely and I can't have that."

"Okay," Gabby says, holding her hands up in surrender. "What are you doing after lunch?"

"I have a full day of pampering ahead," I inform them proudly. "And I'm not going in to the office at all."

"Atta girl," Kate says with a wink. "You deserve a day off."

"I also deserve a mimosa." I grin and search for our waitress so I can flag her down. "In fact, we all deserve a mimosa."

"Excellent plan," Charly says. When we all have a drink in front of us, Charly raises her glass in a toast. "I know we're only focusing on the good today, and every day, and I have to say this."

We raise our glasses with her.

"You're the most amazing person I know, Van. It's been an honor to watch your journey these past couple of years. I couldn't be more proud of you."

"Here, here," Kate says with a nod. "You're one tough bitch, my friend."

I giggle at that and clink my glass to the others. "I'll take that compliment."

"Hell, yes, you will," Callie says before sipping her drink. "There are only great things for you ahead."

"She's right," Mallory says with a knowing smile. I frown and she holds up her hands in surrender. "I'm not reading your future, silly. I can't do that. I'm simply agreeing that you've already been through hell. It's going to get much better going forward."

"I'll take that as well," I reply with a nod. "Here's to a good life."

"A good life," the others happily chime in.

I'M SO DAMN FULL. I forget how I can sit with those women for *hours*, with never a lull in the conversation. We eat and drink and eat and drink and laugh.

So, I'm rushing directly from brunch to lunch with Ben.

I may not be hungry for food, but I wouldn't cancel this date for anything in the world.

I walk into the restaurant we started coming to about a year ago and search the room for him. His back is to me, but I'd recognize him anywhere. He's tall, with super broad shoulders and muscles for days.

For. Motherfucking. Days.

God bless him.

He glances over his shoulder and sees me walking toward him. A smile instantly spreads over his face as he stands and holds his arms open for a hug in greeting.

He's so damn strong and warm, I could stand here in his arms forever. But the hug ends quickly and he holds my chair out for me.

"Hi," he says with a grin.

"Hello there." I glance up to find him studying me

15

with narrowed eyes. "Do I have something on my face?"

"You're flushed." He rubs his lips with his fingertips. "Have you been drinking?"

"Yeah, I just came from brunch with the girls and we may have had a mimosa or four." I giggle and set my menu aside. "I'm so full. I'm sorry, Ben, I can't eat another bite, but you should eat."

"I plan to," he replies. "We could have rescheduled this."

"No, it's okay. I haven't seen you in a while. How are you?"

"I'm good." He nods as he sets his menu aside. The waitress arrives to take his order, and it's a good thing I didn't want anything because she never takes her eyes off of Ben.

The bitch.

She flushes and does a freaking *curtsey* after taking his order, then hurries away.

"You have a fan."

"A what?" he asks, completely clueless.

"Nothing." I shake my head and sip my water.

"How are you today?" he asks.

"I'm fantastic." I grin as he narrows those blue eyes and studies me for a long moment. "I'm not lying."

"I can see that," he says at last, and his shoulders relax, as though he's been carrying the weight of the world on them.

"I need your help, Ben."

"Done."

I cock a brow. "You don't know what I need, exactly."

"Doesn't matter, it's yours."

I grin and lean over so I can pat his hand. "You're very good to me, you know."

"I know." His smile is smug and happy. "What do you need, Vanny?"

"Well, I need you to stop calling me Vanny."

"Not gonna happen."

"And I need to know who you go to for your tattoos."

He spits the sip of water he's just taken and begins to cough, choking.

"Whoa, are you okay?"

"That's the last thing I expected to come out of your pretty little mouth."

Just the way he says *pretty little mouth* makes me break out in a sweat.

Why, for the love of all that's holy, am I so damn hormonal around this man? It must be a chemical response. I was never good at science, but that has to be it.

"I'm serious," I reply and will my lady parts to stand down. "I already have a design in mind, but I don't know where to go."

"Is this your first tattoo?" he asks.

"No," I reply. "But I didn't get mine here in New Orleans."

17

He leans toward me, giving me his full attention. "Where did you get it?"

"In Tennessee."

"No, I mean, where is it on your body?"

I bite my lip and shuffle the silverware around on the table. "That's personal."

"Look at me."

I comply and almost melt into a puddle at the sweet smile he's giving me.

"You can tell me."

"So, tramp stamps were in when I was in college."

"You have a tramp stamp?"

"No, I just said they were all the rage when I was in college."

He blinks slowly, as if I'm not making any sense and he's trying to keep up. "Okay."

"But I thought it looked painful to tattoo the low back, and while I understand that no tattoo is a walk in the park, I didn't want to do it in that spot. Also, I didn't want my dad to ever see it, and sometimes I wear a bikini."

"You do?" He frowns.

"Yeah." I nod and brush it off like it's not a big deal.

"So where is it, Van?"

I bite my lip again. "On the back of my neck."

"And your dad never saw it?"

"No, I've always had longer hair, at least long enough to cover my neck, and I just made sure I didn't wear ponytails when I was with him."

"You're a rebel," he says with a smirk.

"A respectful rebel," I reply. "Will you give me your guy's number?"

"I'll do better than that. I'll take you."

"No."

I'm shaking my head vigorously.

"Why not?"

"I don't want you to see me get this tattoo."

"Why?"

"I just don't."

"Okay, I'll text you his number."

"Thank you."

"What are you doing after this?"

"I'm going to get my hair cut."

*I'm so fucking excited!*

He frowns again. "Why?"

"Because I'm a grown ass woman and I want to."

"Whoa," he says, sitting back and holding his hands up in surrender. "Do whatever you want with your hair."

"That's the plan. I know you like it better long."

"I didn't say that."

"You did when I was fifteen," I murmur and smile at the memory. "But it's okay. It's my hair."

He tilts his head to the side, watching me. "Did that asshole make you wear your hair long?"

*I will not cry today.*

"He made me do a lot of things."

His eyes flare with anger and he pushes his plate

away. "He deserved much more than what I gave him that day."

After Lance tried to kill me, the coward ran. My brothers and the police were looking for him, but Ben found him first.

And beat the fuck out of him before making him turn himself in to the police.

"He doesn't even matter," I reply softly.

"No. He doesn't." He sighs and reaches over to touch my hand. "I'm proud of you."

"I didn't do anything."

His blue eyes hold mine. "Yes, you did. You didn't just survive, Van. You thrived. You're the strongest person I know, and I'm damn proud of you."

*I will not cry today.*

I smile brilliantly at this incredibly handsome man who also happens to be the sweetest I've ever known.

"Thank you. That's the second time I've heard that today."

"You're welcome. It's fucking true." He stands, throws some cash on the table, and holds his hand out for mine. "Let's go."

"Where?"

"I just want to walk with you for a little while."

"Okay."

We don't say much as he leads me through the Quarter and past Café du Monde, then over to the river. It's still early enough in the season that there aren't swarms of people everywhere.

It's actually relatively quiet today.

"Are you okay?" I ask and slip my hand into his, enjoying the zing of electricity as it makes its way down my spine. "You're quiet."

He glances down at me, then out to the water, taking a deep breath.

"I'm great. I just like being here, with you."

"Me too." I lean my cheek against his hard bicep and watch the birds fly over the river. "Me too."

"YOU'VE BEEN COMING to me for seven years," Mandy, my hairdresser, says several hours later. I'm sitting in her chair, the ugly black cape buttoned around my neck. "You've never wanted anything more than a trim on the ends."

"I know, and I hate it."

"Why didn't you say so?"

"Because it wasn't your fault," I reply immediately, not wanting to hurt her feelings. "You've always done a great job. It's the style I hated, but *he* wanted my hair that way."

"It's been two years, sugar. Why are we just doing this now?"

"I guess I just didn't feel healed enough until now," I reply honestly. "It's time."

"Okay." She blinks back tears.

"We are *not* crying today," I inform her sternly.

21

"Right." She clears her throat. "Okay, what do you want me to do?"

"I want you to do whatever you want." I smile, excitement spreading through my chest. "Let's do some color, and a totally different cut."

"I'm so excited," Mandy says, clapping her hands. "I know *just* the thing. Are you sure you trust me with this?"

"Absolutely." I take a happy deep breath and close my eyes. "Let's do this."

For the next few hours, we chat about our families and our jobs. She paints stuff on my hair, then folds it into aluminum foil. I look like I could receive satellite signals.

"Okay, we're going to wash this out, and then I'll cut."

"Great."

The washing part is always my favorite. Mandy gives a kick ass scalp massage. When we return to the chair, she turns me away from the mirror.

"You don't get to see it now until I'm done."

"Okay." I hold my fist out to bump hers, so excited to see what she comes up with. The blow dryer is loud, so we can't chat while she blows my hair dry, and I let my eyes drift closed, happily dozing in her chair. Finally, she snips her scissors through my hair, instantly making it so much lighter.

She puts the finishing touches on it and turns me to the mirror, and all I can do is sit and stare in awe.

"Wow."

"Oh no," Mandy says with horror. "Do you hate it?"

"No." I turn my head to each side, enamored with the sleek, straight black hair with subtle highlights. The ends of my hair barely reach my shoulders now and it frames my face beautifully. "Oh, Mandy, it's so pretty."

And now, despite telling myself over and over again that I wouldn't cry today, I let the tears come.

Because this is the last big step to getting *me* back.

"I am so happy for you," she whispers and catches my gaze in hers in the mirror. Tears fill her pretty brown eyes. "I don't think you'll ever really know how happy I am that you're okay."

"Thank you." I clear my throat and blink the tears away. "I love the way it feels. It's so much lighter, and so soft."

"You have beautiful hair," she replies, running her fingers through it again. "And this length is perfect on you."

She takes the cape off, and I stand, immediately hugging her close. "Thank you so much."

"Thank *you* for letting me play. That was a lot of fun."

I pay Mandy, including one hell of a tip, and practically bounce all the way to my car. I turn the music up loud as I drive home, completely content and happy.

I smile as I pull into my driveway less than thirty minutes later. Declan is here, probably putting the finishing touches on the crown molding in my home office.

"Hello?" I call out as I walk into the house. It's a smaller place, especially compared to most of the others in this exclusive neighborhood. But it's just me, and I don't need a ton of space.

"In the office!" Callie calls out. "We came to finish the molding."

"Good, it's about time."

Declan slowly smiles and looks me up and down. "Nice hair."

"Oh, I love it," Callie agrees.

"Me too." I touch the ends of it, still not used to it being so short. "It was time."

"Damn right," Declan says. "So you had a good day?"

"A great day."

He nods, but I can read his mind. I know my twin brother inside and out.

*Are you really okay?*

I nod. *I'm so okay.*

He sighs. *I still want to kill him.*

*He's not worth it.*

"Okay," Callie says, interrupting us. "Stop it with the voodoo twin speak."

Declan laughs and pulls his wife in for a long, disgusting kiss.

"That's about enough of the gross married speak, too," I say, making gagging noises.

"You love me," Dec says.

"Some days more than others. Like today, when you come to finish my office."

"I can't believe the house is already done," Callie says, propping her hands on her hips and surveying the space.

"It's been a year and a half," I reply, looking at her like she's nuts.

"And we've done the work ourselves," she reminds me. Callie and Declan both love to flip houses, so they've been invaluable.

"I *wanted* to do it myself," I reply. "While I was healing this house, it was healing me too."

I glance around.

"I needed this."

"I know," Callie says and gives me a big hug. "And I'm so glad for it."

"Me too."

"Are you two going to keep chatting, or are we working?" Declan asks.

"Such a man," I say to Callie, rolling my eyes. "He's not great with feelings."

"He has his moments," Callie replies with a smile for my brother.

"I'm sensitive," Declan says with a frown. "But we have a shit ton to do here, and I want to finish today."

"Well, then I guess we'd better get to it." I rub my hands together. "Where should I start?"

"You'll want to change," Callie says. "This might get messy."

"Okay." I nod. "Good idea. You get started and I'll be right back."

I hurry out of the office and down the hall to the back staircase. I pass by the kitchen and have to stop, backtrack, and stare in awe at all of the flowers covering every spare inch of my countertops.

"Holy shit."

"They're from all of us," Declan says from behind me.

"I've never seen this many flowers before."

I can't look at him. If I do, I'll start crying, and I won't be able to stop.

"You deserve pretty things, Van."

"I don't know if I deserve all of this."

He steps up beside me now and takes my hand in his.

"You deserve this and more. You deserve *everything*."

I glance up at him and see tears swimming.

"I think I finally believe you."

"Good." He nods once and folds me into a hug. "It's about damn time."

# CHAPTER 2

*I*t's been an incredible day.

An emotionally exhausting day, but still great.

I sip my wine and stare into my gas fireplace. I know I live in New Orleans, and it rarely gets cold enough for a fire, but I just turn up the A/C and make it work.

Few things are more soothing than a fire.

I take a deep breath and close my eyes. I got to spend this day with everyone I love the most. I ended up running into all of my siblings. And by *running into*, I mean they all took the time to see me.

Even Ben.

And that makes part of me that I thought was long dead sit up and take notice.

Having dinner with Mama was the best way to end the day.

27

The life that Lance tried so hard to kill is alive and well. My house is finished. My family is safe and healthy.

*I* am safe and healthy.

It's taken time, and some therapy, but I've come a long way from that scared, beaten woman that I used to be. It finally feels like that chapter is closed, and I'm ready to see what the next one brings.

Finally, late into the night, I turn the fireplace off, set my empty wine glass in the kitchen sink, and head up to bed.

"OPEN YOUR STANCE, TRACY," Shelly, our instructor, says the next afternoon. I'm in one of my many happy places these days.

Krav Maga has given me so much self-confidence back over the past two years. After *the incident*, Ben added this class to his studio. It's led by a woman, and is for women who've survived physical or mental abuse. It's more than learning self-defense.

It's also about learning self-love and self respect.

"Savannah, don't forget to punch with your first two knuckles."

I nod and punch the woman across from me again. We're sparring today, and it feels fantastic.

Sometimes, a girl just needs to punch something. It's

been as valuable as therapy. For the first year, I pretended I was punching Lance in the face. But now, I'm just punching, protecting myself, getting out some major aggression.

"Better, Van," Shelly says with a nod.

We spend the next hour learning new strikes, and going over the ones we already know. Sometimes I'm the aggressor, and other times I'm defending myself.

It's a fucking amazing workout. My body is screaming at me when the class is over.

"Great job today, everyone. I'll see you next week." Shelly smiles and hugs each of us as we leave the classroom. Shelly also came to Krav Maga about ten years ago after she'd been horribly abused by her ex-husband.

She gets it.

"Van."

I spin at the sound of Ben's voice, and silently cringe. I look *horrible.* I'm sweating like an ice cold drink without a coaster, and the clothes I wear here are skin tight, making it easier to move.

"You're not usually here at this time," I say and dab a towel on my face. "What's up?"

"I had a meeting with another instructor," he says with a smile. "Thought I'd say hi."

"Hi." I smile and readjust my ponytail. It's much smaller now, but I can still pull it back. "How was your day?"

"Busy," he replies and surprises me by letting his

eyes travel up and down my body. "I like the new hair. You look great."

"I'm a mess." I chuckle and hook my towel around my shoulders. "You, however, *do* look great."

That's a fucking understatement. He's in cargo shorts and a black tank top, showing off his tattoos and his muscles.

Good lord, the muscles.

"Can I show you a few things?" he asks, breaking my concentration on his muscles.

"Sure." I frown as I follow him back into the empty classroom. "Am I doing something wrong?"

"No, I just want to go over some form things." He leads me to the center of the room and stands behind me, looking into my eyes through the mirror.

Oh God. This is way sexier than it probably should be.

"Assume the stance."

I follow his directions and work very hard to not react to his strong hands on my sides as he walks me through punches, kicks, and better ways to keep my center of gravity.

"You're small," he murmurs and pushes my legs just a little closer together. "I want you to keep your feet just a little closer together. You'll have better balance."

I nod. "It feels better."

He smiles at me. I can't keep my eyes off of him in the mirror. The way he moves, his facial expressions.

Ben has always been attractive to me, but holy shit,

did he get hotter? Or was I just too broken before to see it?

Because holy shit, he's hot.

"Van?"

"Yeah?"

"I just asked you to do the spin/elbow move."

"Oh." I bite my lip and will myself to stop ogling his arms.

"Are you okay?"

"Of course." I do as he asks and spin, attempting to ram my elbow in his nose, the way I've been taught, but he blocks and sends me onto my ass. "Damn it."

"You're not spinning quickly enough."

"I'm as clumsy as they get," I remind him. "If I spin too fast, I'll fall on my ass. I'll be helping my attacker more than anything."

"It'll actually feel easier," he says, helping me to my feet. "You can do this. I've seen it."

"You're taller than anyone else I've ever sparred with."

"Good," he says and narrows his eyes. "Chances are, if you ever have to defend yourself, your attacker won't be shorter than you."

"True." I nod thoughtfully.

"But if you're still not comfortable doing this with me, that's fine. I can make suggestions for Shelly to work on next week."

"I'm okay," I reply, and am surprised to realize that it's true. It wasn't long ago that I couldn't stand for any man to touch me, not even my brothers. But I don't mind so much now.

In fact, I'm utterly shocked to realize that his touch is turning me on. I don't remember the last time I had sexual thoughts toward a man. Even Ben. Which was one more thing that made me sad.

But hello, long lost hormones.

I wonder if I'm still capable of flirting…

"I can totally do this."

"Of course you can," he says and assumes the stance, waiting for me to hit him.

Or try.

"You know, you should wear more tank tops," I say casually. "Your arms are ridiculously hot."

I spin, faster this time, and actually hit him in the nose with my elbow.

Hard.

So hard, in fact, that he's bleeding.

"Oh God." I stare at him in horror as he covers his nose. "Oh, Ben, I'm so sorry."

He looks…*stunned.*

"That's much better," he says. "Damn, that hurt."

"You're bleeding."

"It's not the first time."

And then, to my fascination, he whips his tank top off in the one-armed way that sexy men do, and presses it to his nose.

But now I can see almost all of him, and I swear, I just started to salivate.

"Wow," I breathe, not able to hide the way my eyes eat him alive from head to toe.

He doesn't just have sleeve tattoos. No, apparently that's just not sexy enough. He has a tat on his ribs, and one on the opposite side, down by that sexy V that travels down under the waistband of his shorts.

"You distracted me," he says. His voice is different now. Rough.

"I did?" I don't think I've ever seen Ben distracted.

"You flirted with me, and that hasn't happened in a while."

"Well, if the end result is you whipping your shirt off, I'll do it all the time."

He frowns, and I realize I've just crossed the line. *He's my brothers' best friend, idiot.*

I shake my head. "Sorry. Really. Won't happen again."

"It's okay," he says. "But I think I need to put some ice on this."

"Come to my place," I blurt out, not at all coy. "You can ice it and I'll feed you. It's the least I can do. I have gumbo in the slow cooker."

He looks hesitant. I'm an idiot. I took it too far.

"Really, I'll keep my hands to myself, and I won't flirt."

"Well, where's the fun in that?" He winks at me. "I'll follow you there."

"Okay." I grin and grab my things. Ben has been to my house before, but never by himself. He came a lot when we were in the throes of renovations to help out, which I loved. It makes me happy to know that the house I love was built by those I love.

The trip to my place is short. I live close to the studio, and not far from Ben. He pulls into my driveway behind me and joins me on the porch.

"It looks different from the last time I was here," he says as I unlock the door.

"It's finally finished," I say with a smile. "Come on back to the kitchen so I can get you some ice. I'm so sorry that I hit you."

"Don't be," he says. "You were supposed to hit me. And I was supposed to block you."

"I can't believe I beat up Ben the Badass."

He cocks a brow as I pass him a bag of frozen peas.

"Who?"

I laugh and take the lid off of the gumbo to give it a stir. "You heard me. I've called you that for years."

"Never to my face."

"Well, no. That would be silly." I smirk and turn to find him leaning against my kitchen counter, the peas pressed to his nose. He pulled on a T-shirt in his car, which is unfortunate because I wanted to look at him a bit more.

"What are you thinking?" he asks.

"That I'm hungry."

"That's a lie." He checks the bag of peas and frowns at the blood. "I told you a long time ago how I feel about lying."

"Well, it's the only answer you're going to get." I reach for bowls and scoop us both up a healthy serving. "Here you go. Do you want to sit in the dining room?"

"I'm fine here." He leans his hip against the counter and takes a bite, then groans in happiness. "I have always loved your gumbo."

*Dear sweet merciful God, that groan.* I automatically clench my legs together as I enjoy the pure lust running through my veins. It feels so good to be sexual again! Even if I don't get to have sex with Ben, at least I know that part of me didn't die.

Although the thought of being touched by anyone else makes me break out into a cold sweat. I know Ben, and I trust him, but he's not the right person for me. And that sucks, so maybe I'm not as healed as I thought.

"Stop thinking so hard," he says and reaches out to tuck a stray piece of hair behind my ear. "How do you feel?"

"Good. Things are really good these days."

"Good." He nods. His nose has stopped bleeding, but it still looks swollen and uncomfortable.

"Are you going to have a black eye?"

"Nah." He shakes his head. "I'll be good as new by morning."

"Of course you will. You're badass."

"Exactly."

I laugh as I take my empty bowl to the sink. I was

damn hungry, but Krav always makes me hungry. I use a lot of calories during that class.

Also, my own shoulders and arms are looking pretty muscular. Not body-builder muscular, but toned enough that I like the looks of my shoulders in a tank top, and that's kind of fun.

Ben joins me at the sink, and we begin to wash and dry our few dishes ourselves, rather than put them in the dishwasher.

"Thanks for dinner," he says as he dries the last spoon.

"Like I said, it was the least I could do after I maimed you."

He chuckles, and then before I know it, he's laughing. Big, loud laughs coming from his belly, and I can't help but join in. We both have tears as we struggle to compose ourselves.

"You're a strong little thing," he says as he catches his breath.

"Well, I hope so. I've been working out for almost two years. It better be doing *something*."

"It's working," he replies and wipes his eyes. "The look of horror on your face was almost worth it."

"Don't make me hit you again."

And just like that, he's laughing again, holding on to the edge of the counter. I grin and cross my arms over my chest, watching avidly. Ben's usually so laid back, so...*calm*, it's rare to see him like this.

And I love it.

I rub his arm soothingly, secretly enjoying the way he feels against my hand. Finally, he takes a deep breath and blows it out slowly.

"I think we both needed that laugh," I say.

"I guess so," he replies and suddenly pulls me in for a hug. An incredible, tight hug, and then he lets go just as quickly. "I'm relieved to see you so happy."

"I think the whole family is," I reply with a nod. "And I get it. But I'm *so* much better, Ben. I feel better than I have in more years than I can count."

"That's all anyone wants." He drags his knuckles down my cheek, sending an electrical current down my spine and arms. I bite my lip, watching his blue eyes as they travel over my face.

He's quiet for a long moment, but finally says, "You're so beautiful."

I blink slowly, wondering if I just imagined that. He shakes his head, as if pulling himself out of a daydream and drops his hand. He walks to the table to retrieve his keys.

"I should go."

"Oh. Okay." I follow behind him as he marches to the front door.

"Thanks for dinner."

He's not looking me in the eyes now, and he's moving quickly, like he can't wait to be out of here.

I never should have tried to flirt with him. I made him uncomfortable, and now he probably feels sorry for me, and the whole fucking thing is just *awkward*.

Which is the very last thing I want between Ben and me. He's my friend. He's practically a part of my family.

We can't do awkward.

"Thanks again," he says and waves as he jogs down to his car. It's a new one. I haven't seen it before. The shiny black of the jeep suits him.

And then he's gone, and I'm left standing on my porch, feeling torn in half. I love him. I've always loved him. But this is *Ben*.

So, I need to get over it. Maybe I should try to go out on a date with someone, just to see if there are any of the same twinges when I'm with someone else.

The thought makes me a bit queasy, but I grab my phone on my way upstairs and call Kate.

"Hello?" The baby is crying in the background. "Eli, can you please take her?"

"It's okay if you can't talk," I say immediately. "We can just text."

"It's fine, she's just fighting sleep. Eli usually has better luck getting her to sleep anyway."

The baby's cries get softer as she walks away from my brother and tiny niece.

"I want to come see the baby soon."

"We would love that. Okay. I'm blissfully alone. What's up?"

"Well, I was just thinking that maybe I should start dating."

Crickets.

I pull the phone away to make sure I haven't dropped the call.

"Kate?"

"I'm here," she says. "I just... are you sure?"

"No." I sit in my chair with a laugh. "I'm definitely not sure, but I think I should at least try. I mean, if it doesn't feel right, I don't have to do it again, right?"

"That's true. And I absolutely love it that you're thinking about this. It means you're in a really good place now."

"Best place ever," I confirm. "But I don't want to date just *anyone*. Certainly not anyone online. I still have trust issues."

"Completely understandable. Hmm, let me think. We know plenty of single men."

"I don't want my brothers to set me up," I reply. "They'd either forbid it altogether, or set me up with someone's grandpa."

"You're so right," Kate says with a laugh. "But they love you, and it's their job to protect you."

"Yeah, yeah. I'm also a grown woman, and I don't need my brothers to play bodyguard. I'm a badass now."

"Yes. You are. Okay. Let me think on it and I'll text you."

"Okay. No pressure and no rush. Really. Because now that we're talking about it, I might feel like I need to throw up."

"Oh, honey, that's perfectly normal for any woman.

Dating is hard work, and it's about ninety percent bullshit."

"Yeah." I nod, even though she can't see me. "Dating sucks."

"Big time sucks. But there has to be at least one guy in New Orleans who is single and not a douche."

"Let's not forget someone who has his shit together. Because frankly, I'm not looking to find someone I have to save or take care of. Just like I don't need anyone to save me. He has to be a productive adult."

"Well, that narrows it down to just about nobody," Kate says with a laugh. "I'm kidding."

"No, you're probably right."

"Let me think— Wait! I know!"

"Okay."

"Oh, what's his name?"

"I have no idea."

"Damn it, I swear, I still have pregnancy brain where I forget *everything.* He works with Simon."

Simon is my sister, Charly's husband. He's a famous British motivational speaker.

"Is he British?"

"I think so."

"No." I shake my head. "No one who lives across the ocean most of the time."

"It's not like you can't afford to go visit him," Kate says, sarcasm dripping from her lips.

"Too much effort. Think of someone else."

"You're awfully picky."

"Damn right I am." I grin. "Every woman should be picky. Which is why I'm so confused as to why you married my brother."

"I heard that," Eli says.

"Stop eavesdropping."

"I'm not, I'm just sitting right next to my beautiful bride."

There are kissy noises, turning my stomach.

"Ew. Get a room."

"We're *in* our room," Eli says with a laugh. "I'll find someone for you to date."

"No. *Fuck* no. Kate, tell him no."

"No," Kate says. "You keep your nose out of this."

"She's my sister."

"I'm going to hang up now," I say, rolling my eyes. "Let me know if you think of anyone. And tell Eli to mind his own damn business."

"You *are* my business, sugar."

"Goodbye," I say loudly and hang up the phone. Good God, what have I done? Now he'll be recruiting my brothers to find me a date too.

Damn it. I should have just kept my big mouth shut.

I shrug and walk into my beautiful new bathroom and run a bath. I strip down and sink into the hot water, lay my head back. I'm ridiculous. Honestly, the thought of meeting a stranger and going out with him, potentially kissing and having *sex* with him makes me want to throw up.

I'm not ready for that. I don't know if I'll ever be ready for that.

Frankly, when I think of being intimate with anyone, it's Ben. It's always been Ben. And yes, the man is so hot he could start a fire at fifty paces. Those muscles, the tattoos, the amazing blue eyes. It's all incredibly hot.

But it's what he is on the inside that pulls at me, almost more so. He's gentle and kind, and when he smiles at me, it feels like everything in the world is just right.

And no one, aside from my Daddy, as ever made me feel that before.

I wonder what Dad would say about all of this. He'd have words of wisdom. I wish there was a phone line to heaven that I could call and speak to him.

But there isn't.

My phone, sitting on the teak tray across my tub, pings with a text.

It's Ben. My heart flutters and I bite my lip as I open his message.

*I'm sorry I'm socially awkward.*

I laugh, relieved that he's making the uncomfortable moment from earlier a joke.

*You're not. I am. And, as it turns out, bad at flirting.*

The three dots blink as he types out his response.

*You're just rusty. Soak those muscles tonight in a hot bath and you won't be so sore tomorrow.*

I grin and snap a picture of my feet resting against

the far side of the tub, just out of the water and send it to him.

*Two steps ahead of you.*

He doesn't reply for a long while, and then finally sends, *Goodnight, Van.*

I sigh, regretting the photo already.

*Good night.*

## CHAPTER 3

~BEN~

"*W*hat the fuck happened to you?" Beau asks as I walk into the gym at Bayou Enterprises. Beau, Eli and I have a standing appointment here three times a week. Their other brother, Declan, sometimes joins us as well, and we talk trash and beat the shit out of each other.

It's my favorite part of the week.

"You should see the other guy," I reply, not answering the question at all. What am I supposed to say? *Your sister, who weighs a buck-ten soaking wet, kicked my ass?*

Eli smirks and jumps up on the pull-up bar to do some pull-ups.

"You look tired," I tell him.

"I have an infant," he reminds me.

"You're wealthy. Don't wealthy people hire nannies?" I already know the answer to this question,

44

but I love getting a rise out of these guys.

"Not these wealthy people," he replies and falls to the floor. "We will hire someone when Kate wants to go back to work, but for now, it's just the two of us."

"I never thought I'd see the day that Eli Boudreaux was not only settled down with one woman, but was changing diapers too."

"It's rather funny," Beau agrees and shrugs when his brother glares at him. "You were always the confirmed bachelor."

"I just hadn't met Kate yet," he says.

"How sweet," I say and laugh when he takes a swing at me. I easily move out of the way, and this begins our sparring for the afternoon. There's little talk involved, other than the typical *don't be a wuss* as we go through the motions of punching, kicking, and generally kicking each other's asses.

"I can't help but notice," Beau says as he steps aside and watches me advance on Eli, "the irony that we did this exact thing when we were sixteen. We just didn't have the disguise of calling it exercise then."

Eli grunts and tackles me around the waist, sending me onto my back. Fatherhood hasn't softened him in the least, and I have to dig deep to get out of his hold.

"Not bad," I say, panting, as I stand and walk to the edge of the mat to get my water. I hear the door of the gym open, and I turn expecting to see Declan, but instead, find Savannah walk in on the sexiest black heels I've ever seen. She grins, then looks at me and her face falls in horror, her skin going white as a ghost.

"Oh my God," she says and rushes to me, those heels clicking quickly on the wood floor. "You said you'd be okay. I gave you a freaking black eye!"

Eli and Beau's smirks aren't lost on me as she moves to touch my face, and I back away immediately.

She can't touch me right now.

Last night at her house was too much for me. I knew I shouldn't have gone, but I couldn't say no. And then she let me touch her, and she fucking *came on* to me, and I had to get out of there before I boosted her up onto the kitchen counter and sunk inside her, making love until I don't know where she ends and I begin.

And that can never happen.

"I'm fine," I reply. "It looks worse than it is."

"Bullshit," she says. I love it when Van gets all fired up. She's so petite, but her size has nothing to do with her attitude. It's good to see this light in her eyes. It was gone for far too long. "You're hurt, and I did it."

"The other guy looks fine to me," Beau says. Tears run down his cheeks from laughing.

"Fuck you," I reply.

"So, how exactly did this happen?" Eli asks.

"He was—" Van begins, but I cut her off.

"It doesn't matter." I walk around her, needing to put some distance between us. "It was an accident. I think we're done for today."

"We still have fifteen minutes left," Eli says with a grin that says he's enjoying the hell out of my discomfort.

"We're done," I repeat. "I'll see you on Wednesday."

"Ben."

I turn at the sound of Savannah's voice and look into her eyes for the first time since she arrived.

"Yeah?"

"I'm really sorry."

She's not just talking about the eye. We both know it. The thing is, she has nothing to be sorry for.

I'm the one who can't handle just being friends anymore. She hasn't done anything wrong, and I hate the thought that I've made her think she has. Which is new to me, because I usually don't give a fuck if I've rubbed someone the wrong way.

But I care about Van.

So I cross to her and kiss her forehead, not touching her anywhere else.

She smells like sunshine and strawberries.

She smells like she used to before her life went sideways.

*Fuck me, I want her.*

"You didn't do anything wrong," I tell her, tipping her chin up. "I'm fine."

She searches my face for a second and then nods. "Okay."

"Okay."

"You're sure you won't stay?" Beau asks. "We have twelve minutes left."

"I'm out," I reply. I'll never make Savannah feel uncomfortable. Well, not intentionally anyway. But I'm smart enough to know when I need to remove myself from her.

I wave as I leave and take the private elevator down and walk to my car, throwing my gym bag in the back.

And my phone rings.

"Hi, Mom."

"Hi, darlin'," she says. She sounds tired. But then, Mom always sounds tired these days. "What are you up to?"

"I just left Beau and Eli and was thinking about heading into the office for a few hours."

"Oh, that's nice. How are the boys?"

I grin. Mom is as much a part of the Boudreaux family as I am. It's always just been Mom and me, but the Boudreaux family was always right next door. My mama and Mama Boudreaux are best friends.

"They're good. I kicked their asses."

"I don't like that language," she reminds me, and I can't help but feel scolded. How is it that no matter how old I get, my mom still has the ability to dress me down with one sentence?

"Yes, ma'am," I murmur. "How are you today?"

"Well, I'm okay, but I was hoping I could talk you into going to the grocery store for me."

I frown. Mom needs help for a lot of things these

days, thanks to all of her health problems, but she's still quite self-sufficient.

"Are you not feeling well?"

"Not great," she confirms. "I haven't been able to get to the store this past week, and I'm out of a few things."

"Of course I'll go," I reply immediately and turn toward her house. She still lives next door to Mama Boudreaux. I think the house is too big for her now, but she loves it, and refuses to move. So I hired a woman to come in once a week to clean for her.

It's the least I can do.

We say goodbye and I make it to her house quickly.

When I walk in, I immediately know that something isn't right.

"Mom?" I call out.

"Upstairs," she calls back.

The house smells of old garbage. She hasn't taken it out in a while, and there are dirty dishes in the sink.

This is *not* normal for my mom.

I take the stairs two at a time and find her sitting on the edge of her bed. She's wearing a robe and slippers. Her dark hair is a mess.

"What's going on?"

"Oh." She waves me off like nothing big is wrong. "I just have a sore toe. I gave myself a pedicure and nicked the skin."

"When is the last time you were downstairs?"

She cringes. "It's been a minute. A couple days probably."

49

"A *couple of days?*" I scowl down at her. "Let me see your toe."

"It'll be okay."

"Mama." My voice is firm.

"Don't you talk to me like that, young man. You may be all growly with your clients and friends, but I'm still your mother and you will speak respectfully to me."

I take a deep breath, pushing the frustration aside. "Yes, ma'am. Can I please see your toe?"

"See, that wasn't so hard," she says. It's a good thing she's looking at her foot as she takes her slipper off rather than my face because she'd tan my hide for the eye roll I just gave her.

But then I look down at her foot.

"Mama, that's not just a sore toe."

The toe is clearly infected, pushing the toes on either side of it out. There's no way she could wear shoes right now. It has to hurt so badly, I don't know how she can bear to walk to the bathroom, not to mention down the stairs.

She still also has several open wounds on her legs thanks to the arterial disease she has that prohibits her body from healing itself. That combined with the diabetes makes it tough for her if she gets hurt or sick.

"Why didn't you call me *days* ago?"

"Because I'm okay."

"Mama, you're not okay."

"I don't want to go to the doctor."

I sigh and scrub my hand over my face. Getting this woman to agree to go to the doctor is like trying to debate with a terrorist.

"I know you don't, but you need to. I'm taking you right now."

"My podiatrist is booked weeks ahead. That's why I gave myself the pedicure rather than go in. A woman needs to have pretty feet."

"I see. Well, then, we're going to the emergency room."

"Benjamin—"

"Mom, we *have* to."

She sighs and finally nods. "Okay then."

I help her dress in sweat pants and a T-shirt, and she wiggles her way back into her slipper, but I can see that it's painful and takes a great deal of effort.

She moves to stand, but I pick her up and carry her down the stairs.

"Well, aren't you just the strong one?" she says with a smile. "Been more than a minute since a man carried me anywhere."

"You shouldn't be walking," I reply and get her settled into the car. "Do you want me to call anyone else?"

"No, they'll probably put me on an antibiotic and send me home. No need to worry anyone."

I hope so.

51

"SHE'S GOING to be here for a couple of days," I say to Beau on the phone a couple of hours later. "They have to amputate the toe immediately, and we're hoping the infection didn't travel up. If it did, there's a chance that she could lose the foot."

"Damn," Beau replies grimly. "I'll be there in just a bit. Are they taking her in for surgery right away?"

"Yeah, they're prepping her now. She's not happy."

"I'm sure not. Just text me which waiting room you're in and I'll be there soon. I'll let the family know."

"I haven't called your mom yet."

"Don't worry, I'll do it. Go be with her while they're prepping her and tell her we all love her."

I grin. "For a guy who can be such a badass, you're sure a softie when it comes to women."

"As far as I know, that's how it's supposed to be," he replies and then he disconnects the call.

I don't know if I've ever told them all how thankful I am for them. Aside from Mom, I don't have any other blood relatives that I know of. If there is family out there, they don't live in New Orleans, and Mom's never mentioned them.

So having the Boudreaux family in our lives has been awesome.

And this is a reminder to me as to why I can't ever try to start something with Savannah. Our families are too linked, our lives interconnected.

I'd never risk losing that.

"There he is," Mom says when I walk into her room.

"Don't tell me you got everyone riled up over this little thing."

"Amputation isn't a little thing," I remind her.

"It's just a toe, Benjamin. Not a whole appendage."

"Thankfully," I reply and lean over to kiss her forehead. "Your eyes are getting droopy."

"They gave me more drugs," she says with a sigh. "I'm so tired of medication."

"I know." I kiss her again and sit next to her. "But I bet you're tired of your toe hurting even more."

"That's true," she says and licks her lips. "Can I have water?"

"Sorry, no," a nurse says as she walks in the room. "We're about to wheel you back. You can have lots of water after you wake up."

Mom grips my hand. "This part makes me nervous."

"You'll do great," I reply and ignore the blatant stares the nurse is giving me. "And I'll be here when you wake up. In fact, I think several of the others will be here too."

"How nice," she says with a smile. "Don't get all fussy with flowers."

"Mom, we like to fuss."

And I know she secretly likes it too, but doesn't want to show it.

Before long she's out cold and another nurse comes into the room to wheel her out.

The first nurse stays behind, and when we're in the room alone, she surprises me with, "I like your tattoos."

"Thanks." My phone beeps with a text. It's Beau letting me know that he's in the waiting room.

"I don't usually do this sort of thing, because it's not exactly professional, but—"

"Please don't," I say, interrupting her. "I don't want to hurt your feelings, and that's all that can come from this conversation."

Her face falls and she nods, then hurries out of the room.

*Shit.* I probably could have handled that more gently, but damn it, they just wheeled my mother back to surgery, I'm beating myself up over Savannah, which is fucking stupid because there's nothing there to beat myself up over, and the last thing I need is my mom's nurse coming on to me.

I mean, who the fuck does that?

I walk out to the waiting room and am surprised to see not just Beau, but Savannah as well.

"How is she?" Beau asks as they both stand.

"She's okay. A little scared, but fine. The procedure should only take about an hour."

"Good," Van says. "Poor Millie."

"She'd been stranded upstairs for a couple of days," I say and drop into a chair facing Beau and Van. "She didn't call me until today."

"Shit," Beau whispers. "She could have even called my mom. She's right next door."

"Stubborn woman," I mutter. "I think I'm going to

have to hire a caregiver to come stay with her. I'm not comfortable with her being alone."

"Do you think she'd go for it?" Beau asks.

"Maybe, especially after this. She may talk a big game, but I could tell that she was scared." I shake my head, frustrated. "I physically carried her out to the car and brought her here."

"Wow," Savannah says, catching my attention. She's listening intently, her eyes full of concern and something else that I've begun to see lately, and don't quite know how to handle it, even though it's like a siren's song that I only want to get closer to.

And that's a bad idea.

"I'm going to go grab us all a coffee at the cafeteria," Beau says and stands. "Do you want anything else?"

I shake my head no just as Van says, "I'd rather have tea, please."

Beau nods and walks away and I'm left alone with Savannah. She moves from her seat to the one right next to me and rubs my arm in firm, soothing strokes.

"She's going to be just fine," she says. "I think the caregiver idea is a good one. Maybe for now all she needs is someone to come be with her during the day. They wouldn't necessarily have to be live in. At least, not for a while."

I nod, unable to talk. Her warm little hand on me is making my dick twitch, and that's not at all appropriate while your mother is in surgery.

But I'll be damned if I can stop it.

55

"Eli's on his way," she continues, her voice soothing and heavy with her accent. "He had to wrap up a meeting and then was going to come here. We called everyone else, and they're waiting for an update. They can be here in a little bit if we need them."

I nod.

"You're awfully quiet," she says and links her fingers with mine, and that's all I can take.

I want to hold her. I want to hug her and not let go. I want to kiss those sweet, plump lips and run my hands all over her little body.

And I want to lie in bed and talk all through the night about nothing at all.

And that's something I've never wanted to do with another woman in my life.

"Shit," I whisper and pull my hand away from her, then deliberately put her hand in her own lap. "I don't think I can do this."

"Do what?" She's frowning.

"You know—"

*Shit, I don't know how to say this.* I take a deep breath and press my fingertips into my eyes, trying to find a way to say this without spilling my guts.

But then it occurs to me that pussy footing around the truth hasn't gotten us anywhere so far, so why not be brutally honest?

"Here's the thing, Van. I can't do this. I can't spend the rest of my life in the friend zone with you."

I stand, putting some space between us and stare down at her. It feels hot in here.

"I love your family, and I owe them a lot. Your brothers are *my* brothers. Gabby and Charly are my sisters, or as close as possible without actually sharing DNA.

"But I don't have those same feelings about you, Van. I don't feel brotherly at all with you."

She won't look at me. Her hands are folded tightly in her lap, and her head is down.

*Fuck me, I'm screwing this up.*

"Look at me." She complies, and her eyes are sad, which is a hard punch to the gut. "I know it feels like this is out of the blue. I just can't sit here and lean on you as a friend, when that's not what I want *at all.* I've had the hots for you since we were kids. But you were way too young for me to try to pursue you, and then our lives just went in two different directions.

"When we were both adults, you got married." I clear my throat, not willing to tell her how much that destroyed me. How hearing those words from Eli brought me to my knees, and the thought of another man having his hands on her made me want to punch the fuck out of someone.

"I know I can't have you, for a million different reasons, and I came to terms with that years ago. But I also can't sit here and pretend that we're just friends."

She doesn't say a word, and she's lowered her gaze again, still not willing to look at me.

Finally, she nods once, stands, and walks away without even a glance back. No goodbye. No punching me for being a dick.

Nothing.

*What the fuck did I just do?*

Not even five minutes later, Eli shows up just as Beau returns with the hot drinks.

"Why did Van just take my car keys and tell me to catch a ride back with Beau?" Eli asks, complete confusion covering his face.

"I just fucked everything up."

Beau frowns and hands me the coffee, then passes Van's tea to Eli.

"Oh no, I get the coffee." Eli reaches for Beau's coffee and hands him the tea.

"What did you say?" Beau asks.

"And how do we unfuck it?" Eli adds.

"You're going to want to punch me."

"That's nothing new," Beau says, his voice as steady as ever. "Spill it."

# CHAPTER 4

~SAVANNAH~

*W*hat in the hell just happened?

I'm driving to Kate and Eli's place. I can't go back to work like this, especially since Kate is still on maternity leave. And I need to talk to her.

Kate's been one of my best friends since she, Declan, and I shared an apartment at college.

I can't believe what Ben just said. He rendered me speechless, and embarrassed.

And not a little bit sad.

I feel tears gather, and I wipe them away furiously.

I am *not* going to cry over the likes of Ben! I'm going to cling on to the anger like a lifeline.

I pull into Eli's driveway and cut the engine, then march up his porch and knock twice before I let myself in.

"Kate?"

"Shh," she says, hurrying out from the kitchen. "I finally got Coraline down."

"Sorry," I whisper. "Is there a safe place for me to rant?"

"Backyard," she says with a nod. She grabs two bottles of cola and the baby monitor and leads me out the back door to the beautiful patio. "Okay. She can't hear us out here."

"I hope I didn't wake her."

She glances down at the monitor and turns it up. "Nope, she's sleeping."

"You have mom super powers," I mutter, making her grin.

"Cool, huh?"

"Pretty cool." I shrug and pace to the edge of the patio, staring at professionally groomed grass and flower gardens.

"What's up?" Kate asks as she settles in a chair.

"Ben," I reply and turn to look at her. "I just left the hospital."

"How's his mom?"

"She was still in surgery when I left."

She narrows her eyes, watching me closely. "He hurt you."

"He pissed me off," I correct her. "I was being supportive. Beau went to get coffee and I stayed with Ben, comforting him, and suddenly, he goes all psycho on me."

"Wait," she says, holding up a hand. "We're talking about *Ben*?"

"Yes. Ben." I march away from her and then back again. "I was just holding his hand, telling him that she is going to be okay, because that's what friends do. That's what *family* does."

Kate nods, so I keep going.

"And then, he suddenly pushes me away and tells me he can't be my friend."

"Wait. What?"

"Exactly!" I point at her. "What the fuck?"

"What did he say? Exactly."

"That he can't pretend that we're just friends anymore."

Her face softens and she sits back in her chair again. "Go on."

"He said he's been attracted to me for years, and he accepts that he's not right for me, but he also can't sit by and just be in the friend zone."

"Poor Ben," Kate says and I scowl at her.

"Why are you on his side?"

"I'm not on any side." She shakes her head and takes a sip of her cola. "But Van, this isn't new news to any of us."

"Well, it's news to me," I reply and finally lower myself into the chair next to hers. "I mean, that's the thanks I get for being a good friend?"

"Okay, pull your head out of your ass," Kate says.

I really want to punch her right now.

"Ben's been in love with you for years, Van. We all know it. Hell, your brothers have been giving him the green light to date you for at least the last year."

I stare at her, stunned. "I don't think I understood you correctly."

"You did." She smiles now. Kate looks fantastic. Motherhood looks good on her.

"I can't be with Ben."

"Why not?"

"Jesus, there are a list of reasons, Kate."

"I'm in no hurry. Let's hear them."

She crosses one leg over the other and waits.

"I shouldn't have come here."

"Yes, you should. I want to hear why you think that you can't be with Ben."

"Okay, there's the little fact that he's my brothers' best friend. That immediately makes him off-limits."

"Except that your brothers have encouraged him to ask you out," she reminds me. "Also, you're not sixteen."

"Kate, he's part of our family. If it doesn't work out, it'll ruin that. We all love him and his mother. I can't risk a lifetime of family relationships just because I want to climb him like a tree and have my way with him."

"Well, Ben's hot, so that's pretty normal if you ask me."

"Gabby and Charly would never think of him like that."

"Gabby and Charly aren't in love with him."

I take a deep breath, and rather than admit to what she just said, I keep talking.

"Also, I'm broken, Kate. I don't know if I could handle him touching me in an intimate way. I mean, I've come a long way, and I find him *so* attractive, but what if in the heat of the moment I can't do it?"

"Well, then you say so and he backs off." She reaches over and squeezes my hand. "Ben would never make you do something you're not comfortable with."

"I know."

"Do you? Because you can't equate love to the bull-shit you were in before. That wasn't even in the same vicinity as love."

"No. It wasn't."

"Besides, when you think of Ben kissing you, do you automatically want to throw up?"

I think back on the previous night at my place and shake my head. "No. Not at all."

"Well, there you go. Besides, Van, you're not broken."

I frown again, but she keeps going.

"You're not broken. You know that I was in a similar relationship before Eli. I thought he'd broken me too, but Eli said something that always sticks with me. He said, *he hurt you, but no one broke you.*"

"My brother can be nice."

She smiles.

"It was the truth. And it's true for you too. You're not broken."

"I can't give him children," I blurt out and then cover my mouth with my hand, staring at Kate in horror.

I've never told anyone this before.

She cocks her head to the side, watching me. "Why?"

I swallow and blink, gathering my thoughts.

"Because *he* hurt me so badly over so much time that I'm infertile."

Her eyes simultaneously narrow and fill with tears.

"I want to kill that motherfucker."

"Well, get in line, because there's a whole slew of us that want the same thing. The point is, even if I could convince myself to risk the relationship our families have, it wouldn't be fair to Ben. He should have kids, and I can't give him that."

"Oh boy," she whispers and pinches the bridge of her nose. "All I've heard from you is excuses, Van. You're making decisions for both of you without asking Ben what *he* wants. You both need to stop being so afraid of each other."

"I just don't know how it could work," I reply softly. "For the first time in *years*, I'm physically attracted to a man, and it's Ben. I'm sure it's because I trust him, and I've known him forever, so it doesn't scare me to think about being with him in *that way*."

"Are you nine? Use your big girl words."

"I want to have sex with the man." I shrug. "I can

admit it. But this isn't someone new who doesn't matter."

"Nope, it's Ben, and that's why I think it's perfect."

I sigh. "I don't think I'm any less confused than I was when I arrived."

"That's okay," Kate says just as little Coraline begins to fuss over the baby monitor. "You don't have to have it all figured out today. I'm sorry he hurt your feelings."

*Is it that simple?*

I guess, at the root of it, that's it. He hurt my feelings.

And I ran off to sulk like a child rather than try to talk to him.

"I have to get the baby."

"Can I come? She won't be little for very long, and I'd love to snuggle her."

"Of course." She leads me inside and to Coraline's nursery. She's sucking on her tiny fist, her feet kicking about.

"She's so dang sweet," I whisper just as she smiles up at me. "And she's a charmer too."

"I'm going to have to lock her up when she's a teenager."

I laugh and reach in her bassinet to pick her up and cuddle her, breathing in the baby smell.

And another smell as well.

"She needs to be changed."

"I think we can trust you to do that."

I wrinkle my nose and look down at the baby. "No peeing on me. Okay?"

She grins again and stuffs her fist back in her mouth.

"That didn't look promising."

Kate laughs as she fetches me a fresh diaper.

"Good luck, Aunt Van."

I'M SETTLED in at home later in the evening, catching up on bills and social media, sipping wine and enjoying the hell out of my fireplace when someone rings my doorbell. It's moments like this that I wish I had a dog. A big dog. Because even though I've come a long way, it would be nice to have the extra protection.

*Pull your big girl panties on and answer the stupid door.*

I peek out the window and frown.

Ben.

He cocks a brow at me and waits patiently. I could walk away, but that's just mean, and I've never been mean.

So I open the door and do my best to block his way inside.

"Hi." He offers me a tentative smile.

"Hello."

"Can I come in?"

"No."

He nods and looks down at his feet.

"Okay, that's fair. But I hope you'll change your mind because I have some things to say."

"Why aren't you with your mom?"

"Because she kicked me out. She said she didn't need me to hover all night long. I'll go back in the morning."

"How is she?"

He smiles. "She's doing well. They only had to take the toe."

"I'm relieved to hear that. But you could have just texted."

"That's not why I'm here." He slaps his hand on the door when I would have shut it. "I'm here about you."

I'm not going to win this fight. He would leave if I got forceful about it, but then I'd kick myself for it later, and wonder what he wanted to say.

So, I turn and walk back into the living room. Ben shuts the door behind him and joins me.

Neither of us sits.

"I really want to apologize."

"Me too," I reply and bite my lip.

He frowns. "Why do you need to apologize? You didn't say anything."

"Well, the thoughts in my head were pretty bad. I might have called you a few names."

His lips twitch with humor, but then he gets serious again.

"I didn't mean to be so blunt earlier, Van."

"Being blunt is better than talking in circles, and far less exhausting," I reply.

"It's hurtful, and hurting you is the last thing I would ever want to do. I want to explain."

"There's really not much to say, Ben. You don't want to be my friend anymore. And I can live with that, but it will make family gatherings a little weird."

"Van—"

"Okay, a *lot* weird."

"No, you're wrong. I *do* want to be your friend. I *am* your friend. But it's also killing me."

He shoves his fingers through his light brown hair and crosses the room to the window, staring through it. His shoulders are wide, his waist lean, and he has the best damn ass I've ever seen.

*Stop staring at his ass.*

He's quiet for so long, I lose patience. "Look, just say what you need to say, Ben."

"We'd be here all night," he says as he turns to look at me. "God, you're so fucking beautiful, Van."

I frown and will the mutant butterflies in my stomach to calm the fuck down.

"I've been attracted to you since we were teenagers." He shrugs. "But you were my friends' younger sister, and there's a code amongst friends that you don't date each other's sisters."

"Is that in a book somewhere?"

He doesn't answer; he just paces the room, talking.

"I knew you were too young for me when I left for

college, and that a relationship at that time in our lives never would have lasted." He swallows hard. "And then, like I said earlier, life just took us in different directions. And then one day Eli calls me and says that you're engaged."

He turns to me now, his face ashen.

"It was the worst day of my life."

"Ben—"

"No, I take that back. It was the second worst day of my life. The worst day of my life was walking into that bedroom after the sonofabitch tried to kill you."

I close my eyes. I have nothing to be embarrassed about, but I hated that Ben saw me like that. It was almost worse than what Lance put me through.

"Look at me," he says and I comply. "I almost killed him, Van."

"I know."

"No." He shakes his head fiercely. "No, you don't know. I *wanted* to kill him with my bare hands. I took so much pleasure in making him bleed. In making him beg me to stop."

*Jesus.*

"I have that in me, and I can't deny that. What I do for a living is violent. And you've already had so much violence in your life, I can't ask you to be mine. I just can't."

"You would *never* hurt me."

"No. I wouldn't. And I can promise you that. But for the first time in my life, on that day, I *wanted* to kill him. And the only thing that made me stop was the thought of going to prison and never seeing you again."

The tears are flowing freely now. I can't stop them. Ben is breaking my heart, and I didn't think that was possible.

"I always thought that just having you in my life was enough. As long as you were happy and healthy, it was enough to be on the outside looking in, but it's just not good enough anymore."

He licks his lips; his eyes are locked on mine.

"You've been a good friend to me."

"Yes. I'm the one you call when you need a ride home from girls' night out. I'm the one you bounce ideas off of. Hell, that's always been the case between us. And I've worked hard to keep my hands off of you."

"What if I don't want you to keep your hands off of me?"

He steps closer as his blue eyes darken with lust. I stand my ground, not afraid of him in the least.

His knuckles gently glide down my cheek as he leans in and kisses my forehead, my nose, the corner of my mouth.

"I'm going to kiss you."

It's not a question, and I'm not going to say no.

I feel like I've waited my whole damn life for this. I know all of the reasons that this can't work, but I'm not strong enough to turn him down.

His lips slip over mine, pressing gently. Ben expertly moves the kiss from soft to passionate, wrapping his strong arms around me as I open up for him, inviting him to explore my mouth and lips, and he doesn't disappoint. I'm drunk from his kiss. The room is spinning, and I have to hold onto his shoulders to steady myself.

Far too soon, he loosens his grip on me and kisses my forehead once again before stepping away altogether.

"Did that feel brotherly?"

"Maybe if we lived in Arkansas," I say as I open my eyes. He smiles and then chuckles, pushing his hand through his hair again.

"I always loved your sassy mouth."

He moves in again, but rather than kiss me, he just hugs me tightly.

"This is what I want," he whispers. "*You* are what I want, Savannah. But it's your choice. I need you to know that this, whatever this ends up being, is your choice."

"I need to think," I reply and bury my nose in his chest, breathing him in.

"You smell good," he whispers.

"So do you."

I pull out of his arms. "I need to think this all over. I need to know that if I can't pursue a relationship with you, I won't completely lose you, Ben."

"You'll never lose me, Vanny."

"You might lose me if you keep calling me that."

He just smiles. "I'm not going anywhere. This isn't

71

an ultimatum. I just have to be honest with you. I think you're finally in a strong place, and I want to be a part of that."

"You already have been."

He nods. "If it helps, your brothers have been trying to talk me into asking you out for a while now."

"So I heard today," I reply. "That's a bit embarrassing."

"Why?"

"Having my brothers beg a guy to date me isn't exactly a good thing."

He smirks. "It wasn't like that at all. They were encouraging. I've never told them everything that I told you today, but they know me. They see how I look at you. They just want us both to be happy."

"They love you," I say softly. "We all do, Ben."

"I know."

"Thank you for coming here to explain things. I needed it. And I need some time to think."

"I figured you would. You always were a thinker." He glances down at my lips, still wet from his kiss. "You think about it, and let me know when you've made up your mind."

I nod, but I already know in my heart what I'm going to do.

I just can't tell him. Not yet. I need to think, and talk to Daddy.

Which I don't mention to him because that'll just make me sound crazy.

"Have a good night."

He nods and walks to the door, letting himself out. I hear his engine roar to life and the headlights make shadows in my living room as he drives away.

I immediately lower myself into a chair, unable to keep my shaking knees under me for another minute.

Ben just kissed the fuck out of me.

And he wants me.

And my family is on board with this.

*Holy shit.*

## CHAPTER 5

~SAVANNAH~

*H*ave I been lying to myself for years? I mean, let's put it all out there on the table. Or, in this case, my bamboo tray that slides over my bathtub. Sitting in a nice, warm bath is usually just the ticket to calm me down.

But nothing is calming me down tonight.

Ben left four hours ago and there is no chance that I'll be sleeping tonight because my brain won't shut the hell up. What am I supposed to do?

If overthink it until I'm sick to my stomach is the correct answer, well, I'm a success.

I did some yoga. I breathed deeply until I thought I was going to hyperventilate. I tried taking a walk but didn't get far because I'm not a big fan of taking walks after dark.

Or taking walks in general.

The bath was my last-ditch effort, and it's not going well so far.

Ben says he can't just be friends with me. That he's had feelings for me since we were kids. But he never said *anything*. Ever. And I definitely never let him know that I had a crush on him.

That would have been humiliating.

Yet, it's still humiliating because according to my family, everyone has known but me.

*What the hell am I supposed to do with this?*

I would have married him in a heartbeat when I was in college. Ben has always been handsome.

Okay, not handsome. Hot as fuck. He's hot as fuck. And only gets hotter with age, which seems unfair somehow.

What would my life have been like if I'd married Ben rather than Lance?

I immediately squash that thought. It's not fair to me *or* Ben. And as horrible as it was, I can't regret it because it shaped me into who I am now, and I really like her.

I fought like hell to be here.

Being Ben's has always been a secret fantasy of mine, but I don't know what to make of it actually coming true. Part of me screams YES! DO IT!

And the other part says *this has disaster written all over it.*

He hasn't given me an ultimatum, he's given me a choice. If I say yes, and Ben and I start to date, and I fall deeply in love with him, it will be catastrophic if and when it all falls apart. I'm not trying to be a cynic, I just have to be realistic because it's not just the two of us at stake. But if I say no, that I want him to back away, and we only see each other at family gatherings, well that sounds like a level of hell I don't want to experience.

Just the thought has my stomach rolling, my chest fluttering, and I'm about a millisecond away from having an honest to God anxiety attack.

"Well, there's your answer, idiot." I take a deep breath and reach for my phone. If I'm going to do this, I'm going to do it *now.*

Before I lose my nerve. But it's two in the morning, and he's probably asleep.

The text is simple. *Are you awake?*

I set the phone down and sigh deeply. No going back now, the text is out there. And really, life is so damn short. Why shouldn't we be together, if that's what we want? We're adults. If the relationship doesn't work out, we can still be friends after.

Probably.

I get out of the bath, the water sliding down my naked body and I remember the way Ben touched me earlier in the day. Gently, like I'm something impor-tant. I wonder how he would touch me in bed.

Holy shit, I'm going to have sex with Ben.

I stare at myself in the mirror and then giggle, holding the towel over my mouth. My eyes travel down my body. I'm thin. Not as thin as I was right after the incident, but still on the thin side. The Krav Maga has given my muscles definition, and my boobs have always been a decent size.

On the down side, I have little bit of a belly that I've never been able to get rid of, no matter how many damn sit ups I do.

I shrug and finish drying off.

Who cares if I have a bit of fat on my belly? If Ben is a man worth being with, he won't care.

And he won't sit in a chair, eating a cupcake, while he makes me do dozens of sit ups.

*We're going to make you thin yet, sweetie. Keep going. I didn't say you could stop. I'll kick you in the cunt if you fucking stop again.*

I shake the memory off, step into fresh clothes, and head to the kitchen. I have left over scones that I bought myself the other day, and I deliberately eat one, at two-thirty in the morning.

*Fuck you, asshole.*

I frown down at my phone. He hasn't replied. Granted, I sent the text two minutes ago. He's probably asleep, but now that I've made up my mind, I want to talk to him *right now*.

I've discovered I'm not a very patient woman these days.

After five more minutes of him still not responding, I decide to just go to his house. I can't imagine that he'd be mad at me for waking him up, especially not with this news.

I can't wait to see the smile on his face.

I grab my keys and bag and head out into the night. It's been raining, so the streets are darker than normal, despite the streetlights. I hate it when it's rained like this. It makes it harder to see.

Thankfully, Ben lives close to me, and I arrive in no time. I only passed a couple of other vehicles on my way.

I park and climb the stairs to the porch of his old home in the Garden District.

There's no answer when I ring the bell.

I wait and ring it again twice, but there's still no movement inside.

"Jesus, does he sleep like the fucking dead?" I ask aloud and walk down to the sidewalk to frown up at the windows on the second floor. I don't know which window is his, since I have never been invited upstairs in his house, so I can't throw pebbles up to wake him.

Besides, with my luck, I would just break the window, and we don't want that. It's not terribly romantic.

I shrug and return to my car. I guess I'll go home and wait for him to wake up. It was silly to just show up here anyway. And this gives me time to really think about what I'm going to say. Because although I've made up my mind that I want to see where a romantic relationship between us will go, I also need to make it clear to him that the most important thing is the family.

Not his sexy arms, or the gentle way he touches me, or the way my heart about flutters out of my chest when I see him.

I turn the corner to my house and frown when I see his car in my driveway.

"What the—?"

I pull in, cut the engine, and sit for a moment, watching Ben. He's sitting on the stairs, his arms braced on his knees, and he's watching me with those bright blue eyes.

I get out of the car and walk toward him.

"Why are you out driving in the middle of the night?" he asks.

"I was at your house," I reply and his lips twitch. "But you weren't home."

"We had the same idea," he says and stands, holding his hand out for mine so he can guide me up the stairs. I'm perfectly capable of walking up the stairs on my own, but I won't ever turn down the opportunity to hold Ben's hand.

He has big hands, but when they touch me, they're the most warm and gentle hands I've ever known

"What was that thought?" he asks.

"I like your hands." I shrug and unlock my door and then lead him inside.

"Van—" he begins, but I turn and wrap my arms around him, hugging him close. "Hey."

"I'm fine," I mutter as he closes the door behind him

79

and loops his strong arms around me, holding me close. "I just needed this."

"It's yours," he whispers and kisses the top of my head.

"Did you get my text?" I ask. He grips my shoulders and pushes me back, a frown on his face.

"No."

"Oh. I thought maybe that's why you were here."

He shakes his head. "I left my phone at home. I didn't hear it go off."

"Then why are you here?"

He licks his lips and slides his hands down my arms to link his fingers with mine. "I couldn't sleep. I couldn't stop thinking about you. I know that I said earlier that this is *your* choice, and it is, but I couldn't stay away tonight. I'm terrified that you'll tell me you can't do this, and if that's what you want, I'll respect your decision. But I needed just one more look at your beautiful face while there's still hope."

My God, how could I have ever considered saying no? His face is ashen. His voice is raw with vulnerability.

He's stripped himself bare for me, regardless of the consequences, and I want with all of my heart to soothe him.

I step to him and cup his face with my hands. His cheeks are covered with stubble, and his skin is warm.

He reaches up to brush a tear from my cheek. I hadn't noticed that I was crying.

"What did you say in your text?" he whispers.

"I just asked if you were awake."

"I am."

I smile and let my hands slide down to his chest.

"I wanted to see you."

He tips my chin up so I'm looking him in the face. "Why?"

"Because it's bad form to tell a man in a text that you don't want to be just friends with him."

He inhales sharply and his hands tighten on mine. "Go on."

"I've always had a crush on you, Ben. Or at least, that's what it was when I was young. You're a sight to behold."

He snorts, but I keep going.

"But more than that, you're so...*good*. You're good, Ben. You've always looked out for me, and made me feel safe."

He frowns, but I keep going, not letting him speak.

"What happened before isn't your fault. I know you beat yourself up about it, just like my brothers do, but it wasn't any of you that caused it. It wasn't my fault either. It was all his fault, and he's being punished for it, Ben. I'm free, and I'm safe.

"You have always been a safe haven for me. So to say that I want to be just acquaintances with you, that I could *ever* be content with that, is just bullshit. I've felt a connection with you for as long as I can remember, and to hear that it's reciprocated is just—" I shrug

81

because I simply don't have a word big enough to explain it.

"Is this a long way of telling me that you want me?" Ben asks, making me laugh.

"Yes. Yes, it is."

"Thank Christ." He pulls me to him again and hugs me so tightly, I don't know where I end and he begins. Finally, he kisses me sweetly, longingly, and all I can do is hold on tightly as he explores every inch of my mouth. When he pulls away, we're both panting, and I would strip him naked right now, but that's not what this moment calls for.

And I'm not convinced that I'm ready for that, anyway.

"Let's sit," Ben says and leads me to the couch. I curl up next to him, leaning my head on his shoulder. He links his fingers with mine and kisses my forehead.

"I have to say something else," I begin. "Ben, if this doesn't work out, it can't change our family dynamic."

"Agreed."

"It's too important."

"I know."

"My brothers would be devastated if they lost you."

"Hey, I just agreed with you."

I sigh. "I know. I just… it's important to me."

"To me too," he replies and wraps his arms around me, tugging me into his lap. "You look so tired."

"I don't sleep much," I reply with a yawn. Now that

we've had our chat, and he's *here*, all I want to do is sleep.

"Drift off," he says. "I'm right here."

"We could go upstairs."

"No, we can't." He kisses my temple. "I don't trust myself in a bed with you."

I pry my eyes open. "That wouldn't be horrible."

"It better not be horrible," he says with a chuckle. "But we're not there yet."

"Almost," I say. "I've had to keep my hands off of you for a very long time."

"Go to sleep," he whispers in my ear. He's playing with my hair, and between that, his warmth under me, and his strong arms around me, I can't resist. I let sleep fall over me.

"Do you need anything before I leave?" Becky, my assistant, asks at the end of the workday.

"No, I think I'm good to go. Thank you."

"Don't spend the night here," she says and narrows her eyes on me. "I'll know if you do."

"I always forget who the boss is in this relationship," I reply with a laugh.

"It's mutual," she says.

"I came in late today. I need to stay late to catch up."

She nods and backs out of the doorway with a wave

and I stretch my neck before returning to my computer.

About an hour later, there's a noise just outside my door.

"Hello?" I call out just as a man walks into my office, a huge bouquet of tulips hiding his face.

But I'd know Ben's legs anywhere.

"Delivery," he says and then looks around the side of the bright pink blooms and flashes a smile at me.

"You're the best looking flower delivery man I've ever seen."

He smirks and sets the flowers on my desk.

"Thank you."

"You're welcome. Are you about done here?"

"Almost," I reply with a sigh. "*Someone* let me sleep late this morning."

"I wasn't even there," he says, holding his hands up in surrender.

"Exactly. And my alarm wasn't set, so I slept until nine, and I don't remember the last time I slept that late."

"You needed it."

"I was late to work."

"You own the business, Van. I hardly think anyone is going to write you up for being an hour later than normal."

"I don't know, Becky looked like she'd thought about it." I laugh and stand, stretching my back and arms, then lean over to smell the flowers. "I love tulips."

"I know."

"You look mighty smug right now, Mr. Preston."

"I'm feeling mighty smug, Ms. Boudreaux," he replies and walks behind my desk to kiss the hell out of me.

Jesus, the man's lips should come with a warning label.

*May cause light-headedness and a loss of control.*

"I have plans for us tonight," he says.

"You do?"

"Yes, ma'am."

I tilt my head. "I'm working."

"It's after work hours."

"But I'm catching up from missing an hour this morning."

"It's two hours past working hours. You've made up the time. Unless you don't want to see what I've planned, and trust me when I say, you want to see it."

"Does it involve food?"

I'm suddenly *starving.*

"Oh yeah."

"I'm in."

He laughs as I shut my computer down and gather my things. He takes my handbag from me and smirks when I glance up at him in surprise.

"I don't mind carrying my own handbag."

"There's no need for you to carry it."

"You're either very chivalrous, or you're a control freak."

His face changes, and I immediately regret my choice of words.

"I didn't mean it like that. At all."

"I know. I'm not trying to control you, I'm just carrying your bag. I plan to do lots of nice things for you, Savannah. And that's all it is."

"Thank you." We step into the elevator and when the doors close, I kiss his bicep. "Really. Thank you."

"You're welcome."

"Is this our first official date?" I ask, getting excited all over again.

"It is," he says. "I've waited fifteen years to take you out on a date, so I might have gone a little overboard with this."

I raise a brow and suddenly can't wait to see what he has up his sleeve.

"You do know that you're incredibly sweet, right?"

"With you, that seems to be true. But you can't tell your brothers because they think I'm badass, and if this gets out, I'll have to kick their asses extra hard in the gym."

I laugh and follow him out of the elevator toward his car.

"Thanks for texting me the name and number of your tattoo guy," I say once we're settled in the car. "Is his given name really Buck?"

"I don't know; he's a man of few words, but he does a great job with ink."

"That's all that matters, I guess."

"What are you going to have him do?"

I bite my lip, not sure if I want to share that yet. "You'll see it when it's done."

"Do you have an appointment?"

"Yep, I'm going in on Saturday morning."

He glances over at me in surprise.

"What?"

"Buck usually closes on Saturdays."

"He said he'd fit me in." I shrug. "I might have offered to pay double."

Ben laughs and nods. "That would do it."

Before long, he parks in front of a cooking school.

"Are they running a special tonight?" I ask.

"You'll see."

He leads me inside and to a kitchen where a woman tastes something from a pot. She's in a white jacket and a tall white hat.

"Hello," she says with a kind smile. "You must be Ben."

He nods. "And this is Savannah. Van, this is Chef Baker."

"Hello." I nod and smile inside when Ben takes my hand firmly in his.

"Well, you are my only students this evening," Chef says with a smile. "Welcome."

"Students?"

"That's right," Ben says. "We're going to learn to cook a meal together."

I blink at him for a moment and look around at the

87

industrial kitchen. It's spotless, full of stainless steel, and ingredients are already waiting for us on the countertop.

"Great. What are we making?"

"BBQ shrimp, grits, and bananas Foster," Chef replies. "I hope you're hungry."

"I'm so hungry."

I glance up at Ben, who's been watching me intently.

*So hungry.* And not just for food.

## CHAPTER 6

~BEN~

*J*'m on a date with Savannah. A second date, if we want to get technical. Our first date last night was more fun than I anticipated. I knew that Van already knew how to cook, but I don't, and I thought it would be something fun to do together.

She smiled all evening.

And now, the morning after, I've picked her up and we're at her favorite breakfast spot before we each go to work.

"Thanks for getting up extra early to do this," she says as she studies her menu.

"If I have to choose between you and sleep, you win every time, sugar."

She smiles sweetly and returns to her menu. "You did well last night."

I snort. "I almost killed us both with the knife."

She wrinkles her nose and then busts up laughing.

"You didn't almost kill us. But I was worried that you might take off a finger for a second there."

"I think it's best if I stay out of the kitchen. I'm not saying that in a sexist way at all."

She's chuckling behind her hand.

"I think I'm destined to eat take out for the rest of my life," I say.

"I'll cook," she says, waving me off. "Not because I'm a woman, but because I like to."

The waitress arrives to take our order, and Van accidentally catches the water glass with her menu, pushing it forward and spilling all over the table and my lap.

"Oh my God," she says, her eyes wide with fear. "Oh, I'm so sorry. I'm so, so sorry."

"It's okay," the waitress and I say at the same time.

Van's fingers have started to shake. "I am so stupid. I'm sorry, Ben."

"Hey, it's an accident."

She's shaking her head, not hearing me at all. The waitress quickly cleans up the water and ice cubes and passes me an extra napkin to wipe up most of the water on my pants.

"Hardly any of it fell on me," I say. But Van is shaking, an anxiety attack moments away. I turn to the waitress. "Give us a minute."

"Certainly," she says and marches away. I reach over to take Van's hand firmly in mine. "Savannah."

"I didn't mean to do that."

"Look at my face, baby."

Her eyes find mine. They're full of tears and fear and every muscle in my body tightens in pure fury.

*That fucker put this in her.*

"Savannah, it's okay." My voice is calm, belying the blood rushing through me. I'd love the chance to have another go at that asshole. "Do you hear me?"

She nods, watching me with wide hazel eyes. Her hand is clinging to mine for dear life.

"Listen to my voice."

"I like your voice," she whispers.

"I like your voice too." I smile gently and pull her hand up to my lips, kissing her gently. "You didn't do any harm. It's cleaned up, and it barely got me."

"I'm so embarrassed."

"Take a deep breath."

I keep her gaze locked on mine as I take a deep breath, letting it out slowly. On the second one, she joins me. The trembling has stopped.

"See? You're great."

She bites her lip and squeezes her eyes shut for a moment, and then I watch in wonder as she physically makes herself calm down, most likely using whatever tool her therapist has given her.

Jesus, she's strong.

"I've been told I have some PTSD."

"That makes sense," I reply and take my own advice, breathing in deeply. "Does it happen often?"

"Not anymore," she says and takes a sip of the fresh

water the waitress delivered. "It used to happen all the time, but now it's sporadic. I never know what might trigger it."

"I think that at some point, not today, but sometime soon, we should talk about the worst of it, so I know what may or may not upset you."

"You don't have to treat me like I'm made of glass."

"Did I just say that?" I ask.

"No."

"You're not glass. You're fucking badass, Van. But part of my job as your man is to protect you, and if you think I won't do whatever I have to to keep this from happening again, you're mistaken."

She blows out one last burst of air and picks her menu up, signaling for the waitress.

"Okay, Captain America. You can protect me."

"I think I'm better looking than Captain America."

She narrows her eyes as if she's studying me over the top of her menu. "I'd say it's close."

I cock a brow, but the waitress interrupts us.

"Are you ready to order?"

"Yes," Savannah says. Her voice is strong again, and she's the confident, beautiful woman I've always known. "I want the sweet potato pecan waffles with a side of bacon."

"And to drink?"

"Coffee is great."

"And you, sir?"

"I'll have the same, but make mine a double side of bacon."

She takes our menus and leaves, and my hand immediately finds Van's again.

"I have to go to a gala tonight," Van says with a wince. "I get shy at these things, but we're celebrating the completion of the contract with Signet Shipping."

"Lance's company?" I ask with a frown.

"Well, it's his family's company, and he's not a part of it anymore, but yes. We're not renewing, given the circumstances, but it was a successful contract. It brought Bayou Enterprises a lot of money and exposure on the East Coast. It's not a huge party, only a couple dozen people will be there, but I have to get dressed up. Will you come with me?"

"Do I have to get dressed up too?"

"God, I hope so," she says with that sexy smile that makes my cock stand at attention. "You look hot in a tux."

"Is that right?"

Van looks me up and down and a smug grin spreads over her face. "Oh yeah. Super hot."

"Are you ready to let your family see us like this?"

"I'm a grown woman, and I'm not ashamed of you. They're going to see us together sooner or later. Why wait?"

"Hey, I'm totally on board with that. I just want to go at your pace."

"I'm comfortable here," she says. "And I am excited to see you dressed up."

"Likewise," I reply. "You're stunning in a formal gown."

"I even bought a new one," she says, winking at me. "I've decided it's time to show off the girls."

I choke on my water as Savannah smiles smugly.

"I'll never complain about that."

"Good." She says and sits back as her food is placed in front of her. "You can pick me up at six."

"Shouldn't I take you to dinner first?"

"That's why you're picking me up at six," she says and takes a bite of her bacon. Jesus, she's gorgeous. The bad moment from a bit ago is over, and she's now in full-on flirt mode.

My dick is already semi-hard, as if I'm seventeen and a girl just told me her parents are gone for the weekend.

But I'll happily control myself until she's ready. This is a marathon, not a sprint.

"What are you thinking?" she asks.

"That you're sexy as hell."

She blinks twice and then laughs. "Just wait until you see my new dress."

"You'd be gorgeous in a burlap sack."

"Back at you," she mutters and pours syrup on her waffles. "Does it bother you to know that I'm just with you because you're arm candy?"

She bites her lip, trying to keep a straight face. She's teasing me.

"I can live with it if you can."

"Oh, I'm living with it, handsome."

She takes another bite of bacon and winks at me.

I'm in so much trouble.

"YOU'RE STUNNING," I whisper into Van's ear for the third time this evening. She wasn't lying when she said the new dress showed off her tits. Her cleavage is impressive, but the dress is still classy.

The shoes, sleek and black and boosting her up at least five inches, are sexy as fuck. I would love for her to wear them and nothing else, her legs wrapped around my shoulders.

And we'll get there.

"I think you might be biased," she says with a grin. She's been sipping on the same glass of wine for the last hour. She clearly doesn't want to get drunk in front of colleagues, and that's just one more reason to respect her.

"Not at all," I reply. She's been holding onto my hand all evening. None of the family have commented, but there have been some knowing smiles thrown my way.

"Van?"

We twirl at the sound of a man's voice, and I have to physically hold myself back from throwing a punch.

"Larry?" Van frowns. "I didn't know you'd be here."

"I just flew in," he says with a smile way too much like his twin brother's. He leans in to kiss Van on the cheek and turns to me, holding his hand out for a shake. "Ben, right?"

Van elbows me, and I shake his hand, but keep eye contact with him.

"Well, I wish you'd let me know you were coming," Van says. "I would have made time for lunch or something."

"No need, it's a quick trip," he replies easily. I know that Van has said a few times that Larry is the opposite of his brother. But frankly, I don't like him.

"I'm so happy that the contracts went so well," Van says. "Eli took over that project for me, and I know you all worked hard on it."

"We did, and it worked out great for all of us," he says with a nod. "I won't keep you. Have a good evening." He touches her shoulder and then walks away and Van takes in a long, deep breath.

"Are you okay?"

"Yeah." She nods and takes a drink of her wine. "I know that Larry is harmless, but it's always a shock when I see him in person. He and Lance look *so* much alike."

"I wanted to punch him just on principal."

She laughs and shakes her head. "He's not the bad guy."

"Do you have a lot of contact with him?"

"No, not anymore." She returns a wave to someone across the room. "He checked in quite a lot in the beginning, but now I only hear from him every couple of months or so. He's a good guy."

I simply nod and welcome the distraction of Beau as he approaches us.

"Hello," he says, a smug smile on his face.

"Hi," Van says and slips her hand back in mine. Beau winks at her, then turns to me.

"It's about time."

"It's the *right* time," I reply. "How late is this scheduled to go?"

"Just about another hour," Beau replies. "People are already trickling out."

"I know you don't love these things," Van says. "Thank you for bringing me. And for wearing the tux. It's seriously hot."

Beau cocks a brow. "I don't think I need to be privy to this conversation."

"I'll take you anywhere," I reply, ignoring Beau altogether. "I'm good for another hour."

Over the next thirty minutes or so, Savannah is interrupted with words of thanks from the guests. She smiles, shakes hands, and is the perfect professional. I can see that she certainly has the respect and trust of her colleagues.

She's pulled away for a conversation with a group of people, and I suddenly have to make a run for the restroom.

Jesus, I haven't been this nauseated since I was a kid. I barely make it there in time to lose my dinner, lunch, and probably what I ate last week, too.

"Fuck," I mutter when I can catch my breath. I fumble for a towel to wipe my mouth and the sweat from my brow.

It doesn't look like I'll make it another half hour.

I spend another few minutes praying to the porcelain gods, convinced that I'm going to die, and then go in search of Van.

"Oh my God," Mallory, Beau's wife, says. "Ben? Are you okay?"

"Not feeling great," I reply and scan the room, finding Van by the door. "I need to get out of here."

"We're on it. Beau!" She waves Beau down and the two of them work to get Van and me out of here. Beau calls down to have the valet ready with my car.

"You're going to have to drive," I say to Van, who only continues to frown and watch me carefully.

"Of course I'm driving," she says. "Can you make it down to the car?"

I start to nod, and then have to make a run for the bathroom. I don't even give a shit that it's the women's bathroom. The only thing that matters is that it's the closest one.

"Should I call an ambulance?" Beau asks behind me.

"No."

"The flu is going around," he says and I shake my head. "Just get me home where I can die in peace."

"You can't do that." That's Van's voice now. "We finally got to the good stuff, so you can't die yet."

"That's a lot of pressure," I whisper.

"Should I ride with you two?" Beau asks.

"Maybe," Van says, uncertainty heavy in her voice. "If he needs help up to his bedroom, I won't be able to assist much."

"Good point."

"No," I say in between heaves. "We can do this."

I hold my hand out and someone puts a cold, wet cloth in it. I wash my face again and stand up. "Let's go."

"I'm helping you out to the car, and if I think you need it, I'll go home with you too."

"I don't care," I reply honestly. I feel like I'm dying. That my insides are cramped so tightly, my body is trying to shove everything out of my mouth.

And, it's succeeding.

Fucker.

"Have you been around anyone who had the flu?" Van asks. She's rubbing circles on my back, and it bounces back and forth between feeling like heaven and the most annoying thing ever.

"I work with hundreds of strangers every week," I remind her. "Probably."

"I'm so sorry," she says as the elevator doors open

and the valet has indeed pulled my car to the curb. Van and Beau help me into the passenger seat.

"Here! Take this," Mallory says, handing me an empty ice bucket. I didn't even know she was with us.

"Are you sure you're okay?" Beau asks.

"We'll be fine," I reply. "I can walk up the stairs to the bedroom. And if I can't, I have a guest suite downstairs that will do fine."

He nods and looks at Van, who's just climbed in the driver's side and is adjusting the seat. "Call me if you need me."

"I will," she promises and starts the car.

"It feels weird to have someone else drive my car."

She reaches over and pats my leg. "I'm so sorry this is happening. You look miserable."

"I feel miserable." I can feel my stomach muscles begin to contract, so I push the button to roll the window down. The cool air feels good on my face. "I feel drunk."

"And you didn't even get to have the fun part to get there," she says. Her voice is throaty and smooth, and it soothes the rough edges of this hell.

It feels like it's taking forever, and the cool air isn't doing the trick anymore.

"Pull over."

"We're—"

"Pull the fuck over."

She complies, and she isn't even at a full stop when I

open the door and practically roll out of the car to the curb and hurl some more.

Jesus, how do I still have anything in me?

Suddenly, Van is behind me, pulling the tux jacket off. That feels much better. I'm hot and having the chills, all at the same time.

Finally, I dump myself back in the car and Van drives us to my place. I'll feel like an ass tomorrow, but I can't wait for her. I have to hurry or I won't make it.

I run up the stairs to my bedroom, stripping out of my clothes along the way, and head right for the master bathroom.

"I'm behind you!" she calls out. I can't reply, I can only kneel on the cold tile, in my underwear, and heave into the toilet.

What the fuck do I have?

Finally, I just collapse on the floor, shivering, but loving the way the cold floor feels against my hot skin. It feels too tight, too hot.

I'm sweating like crazy.

"In the shower," Van instructs and helps me into the standing shower. I'm upright, leaning on both hands against the tile. She turns on the water and I don't even flinch at the burst of cold water.

"Too hot," I say when it starts to warm up.

"I don't want to give you hypothermia."

"Please, it's too hot."

She complies, turning it to the coldest setting, and I

can finally feel my stomach and organs begin to relax. I think the worst of the throwing up is finally over.

"Worst hour of my life," I mutter.

"It's only been thirty minutes," she informs me. "If you're not feeling any better, I'm calling an ambulance."

"I am," I say and reach blindly to hold her hand, giving it a squeeze. "You're an angel."

"I wouldn't go that far."

I glance over at her and frown. She's sopping wet in her sexy new dress. Her feet are bare.

"I ruined your dress."

"It's just a dress," she says soothingly.

"How are the shoes?"

"They're fine. I took them off when you made me pull over."

"Good. I like them."

She kisses my bicep. "I'm not leaving you tonight."

"Good. I don't want you to. You're safe from my sexual advances tonight."

She smirks. "I don't think I'm ever in danger with you."

"I'm too weak to argue."

"You stand here. I'm going to go pull your covers back and get you something cold to drink. Oh, and fresh clothes."

"I'll sleep naked," I reply. "I'm so fucking hot."

"The water is ice cold."

"Must be one hell of a temperature."

"I need a thermometer," she mutters.

"I have one in the medicine cabinet."

"Great. Wait here for me, and I'll help you to bed."

She leaves, and about ten seconds later, I turn off the water and dry off, peeling out of my wet underwear.

I'm not going to make her help me to the bed. I'm not a fucking invalid.

I grab a fresh pair of underwear, deciding not to give her the shock of her life tonight, and climb under the covers.

"So, you're not great at taking direction," she says as she comes into the room.

"Nope."

"So noted," she says and sticks the thermometer in my ear. "Jesus, Ben."

*That's what I want her to say when I'm inside her.*

"You have a fever."

"That I knew, sugar."

She grins down at me, and I swear to God, she's a fucking angel. An angel that I don't deserve, but I'm so damn grateful for.

"But it's not going to kill you."

"Feels like it."

"I know." She kisses my forehead and then places a cold towel over it and I want to just ask her to marry me. "Go to sleep, Ben. I'll be here when you wake up."

*I want you to be here every time I wake up.*

103

# CHAPTER 7

~SAVANNAH~

*D*id I do the right thing?

He's restless in his sleep, and he won't stop sweating. I Googled his symptoms, and that about gave me the anxiety attack of the century.

Basically, he could have the flu or he could be dying from organ failure.

Or about a million other things.

The most logical is the flu.

My phone vibrates next to me, making me jump a foot in the air.

"Hi, Eli."

"How's Ben?"

"I think he's doing better," I reply, my eyes never leaving the man in question. "He's not throwing up anymore. But he's sweaty and he looks super uncomfortable while he's sleeping."

"You're staying with him?" I can hear the unspoken question in his voice.

"Yes, and no, I'm not in the bed with him, but if I was, that would be our business."

"Geez, I didn't even say anything."

"You're my brother; you were thinking it."

"Honestly, Van, I wasn't thinking that at all. I was thinking, it's about damn time my sister starts to do what makes her happy. You looked happy tonight. Truly happy for the first time since you were a kid."

I bite my lip, relieved that he can't see the tears fill my eyes.

"I'm happy."

"And Ben looks like he's the happiest man in the world. He actually smiled tonight, and that man never smiles. That's all any of us ever wanted for you, Van. For both of you. And, we know and trust Ben."

"I know you do."

"So none of us will flip you any shit for this. It's been a long time coming."

"Thank you."

"You're welcome. Now, does the pinhead need a hospital?"

I grin at the term of endearment, which is exactly what that was in guy-speak.

"I don't think so. He's settling down. But if he gets worse again, I'll call an ambulance and let you know."

"You do that." He sighs and I can hear the baby cooing in the background. "Be happy, Sis."

"You too."

I hang up and let the tears come. These aren't sad or scared tears. They're relieved and grateful tears.

My family is the best there is.

I wipe my face and walk over to Ben. It's time to check his fever again, and I don't want to wake him. I gently push the thermometer in his ear and click the button.

It's coming down, thank God.

"Vanny," he whispers and catches my hand in his. He hasn't opened his eyes.

"Yes, sweetheart."

"Oh, that's nice."

"The cool rag on your neck?"

"No, you calling me sweetheart."

I sit on the edge of the bed next to him and lean over to kiss his forehead. He's not sweating anymore.

"Are you still shivering?"

"No. Better."

"Good," I whisper. "You scared me there for a minute."

"Scared me too."

I push his hair back with my fingers. The light brown strands aren't overly long, but they are soft, and they feel good against my skin, so I keep brushing it back.

Honestly, it just feels amazing to be able to touch him whenever I want to.

"Van?" he says.

"Yes, sweetheart."

His lips turn up at the sides, and I make a note to call him sweetheart regularly.

"I don't want to get you sick, but I'm so glad you're here."

"I won't get sick," I promise him and kiss his rough cheek. "Don't you know? If you're tending to the sick, you don't get sick yourself."

"That's bullshit."

I grin. "Well, yeah, but that's what I'm telling myself."

"Will you please sleep next to me?"

I nod, but realize he can't see me.

"Of course."

I walk around to the other side of the bed. I'm wearing a T-shirt and boxer shorts of Ben's that I found to change out of my sopping dress. I climb in next to him and spoon up behind him, kissing his shoulder. I'm not going to crowd him all night, but it feels amazing to snuggle up next to him.

"Goodnight, Ben."

"Goodnight, love."

*Oh boy.*

Could this be happening too fast? I'm sure that some would say yes, but frankly, I feel like it's always been here, and I had blinders on.

Or, I was married to someone else for a long time, and then too broken to even want to feel anything for a man again.

But the wounds are healed, and Ben had a lot to do with that recovery.

I've known him most of my life.

So, no, I don't think I'm rushing things to admit to myself that I'm in love with him. Am I ready to say that to him yet? No. I'm not.

But I'm never going to lie to myself again.

I love Ben.

*I HATE THIS GODDAMN DREAM. This is why I don't sleep well. Ever.*

*I'm walking along the shore of the river, letting tall grass brush over my hands. It's sunny, but not too hot. It's a nice day.*

*But suddenly, the sky is filled with dark clouds, moving ferociously and tossing lightning back and forth. I need to get away from the river, to somewhere safe. So I run away, just as it starts to rain.*

*I know what happens next, and my heart is beating so hard, I'm convinced it's going to come right out of my chest.*

*Don't go for that cabin. Horrible things are in there. Don't do it.*

*But just like always, I run inside the cabin, trying to escape the storm.*

*I shut the door and look about, and there, next to a roaring fire, is Lance.*

*His face splits into a smile. An evil, spiteful smile.*

*"There you are. I didn't give you permission to go out for a walk."*

*"I didn't go far," I reply and immediately put my head down. Lance prefers for me not to look him in the eyes.*

*"It doesn't matter how far you went; you didn't ask for permission."*

*"I'm sorry."*

*"You know what to do."*

*I clench my eyes closed and lift my shirt, turning my back to him. I hear the crack of the whip, but it doesn't hit me.*

*"Where did you go?" he yells and I turn around, hope blooming in my chest. "Savannah?"*

*He can't see me. I drop my shirt and move carefully, in case it changes, but it doesn't. He can't see me. He's yelling for me, his eyes crazy the way they get right before he beats me extra bad.*

*So I turn and run out of the cabin and back into the storm. I don't know where to go. He brought me here, and I don't know how to get back home.*

*The wind is frantic, sending my long hair in a frenzy, covering my face. I can't get it out of my eyes.*

*Oh, God, I can't see!*

*"Savannah!"*

*He's come outside, and he's running after me. Why can he see me again? Why is the dream going like this?*

*"Stop it."*

*It's my daddy's voice.*

*"Savannah, you stop this right now."*

*I open my eyes and sit up and there he is, my daddy, sitting in the chair by the window.*

*"Daddy?"*

*"Hi, pumpkin." I smile, despite the breath heaving in and out of me. Ben is still sound asleep.*

*"What's happening?"*

*"You're having that damn dream again, and I won't have it." He leans forward, his elbows on his knees. "Savannah, the dream is your own doing."*

*"It's just a dream. I don't have control over my dreams."*

*"You are still letting him mess with you, and this is where it stops, baby girl."*

*Humiliating tears fill my eyes. "You can see all of that? Do you know what he did?"*

*"Yes," he replies. "I wish you'd come to me when I was still here to help you."*

*"He threatened to kill all of you. To destroy the company."*

*"He's a smarmy little sonofabitch who couldn't have done any of those things."*

*"I know that now, but I was afraid that he was telling me the truth, and I couldn't bear the thought of him hurting any of you."*

*"So you bore the burden yourself. That's not what we do in this family, Savannah."*

*I nod and Dad holds his hand out to me. I rush out of the bed and climb into his lap the way I did when I was small and afraid.*

*"I miss you, Daddy."*

"I know," he says. God, he smells the same. His arms feel the same. It's like he's really here, and it's not just a dream. "I miss you too. And I'm so proud of you, baby girl. You've done an amazing job of healing and moving on."

"Then why do I still have that horrible dream?"

"Because the past is always with us, even when we think we've moved on. There's something, even if it's in your subconscious, that's still afraid of him."

"I don't know what it is."

"You don't have to. But you do need to sleep peacefully, daughter. You've sure earned it."

I lean my head on his shoulder and take a deep breath, feeling sleepy again.

"I used to love to sleep on you, just like this."

"Yes, you did."

"Can I now?"

"You're here, aren't you?"

I smile and cup his cheek in my hand, the way I used to. And, like I did when I was young, I fall asleep in my daddy's arms.

"Did you ever look into getting a caregiver for your mama?" I ask Ben three days later. We're in his car, driving toward the bayou.

"Yes, and already found someone," he says. He recovered quickly from the bug he had the other night.

111

He says that he usually recovers quickly from illnesses, thanks to his lightning fast metabolism.

I wish I had a lightning fast metabolism.

"That was quick."

"I mentioned it to Becky—"

"My assistant?"

"Yeah, I mentioned it to her about a week ago when I called for you and she asked how Mom was before patching me through to you. She knew someone at an agency, and put me in touch. I found a nice lady named Sally who's about ten years younger than Mom, in great shape, and she comes during the day from breakfast until after dinner. She's great, and Mom even likes her."

"Your mom likes everyone." I grin at his profile, enjoying the way the sunshine sets off the stubble on his face. He's just so ridiculously handsome.

"Yeah, she does. I feel better knowing someone's with her."

"I'd like to meet Sally," I say and stare out the window. "You know, check her out for myself. I love Miss Millie."

"We'll stop by there tomorrow," he says and takes my hand, lifting it to his mouth to give it a kiss.

My stomach flips over every time he does that, and it happens quite often, much to my delight.

"So why are we going out to the inn?"

"I promised Rhys I'd help him with some things."

I frown at him. "Rhys usually hires out a lot of the

manual stuff. Not because he can't do it, but he'd rather make sure someone licensed does everything in case they ever have to file a claim with the insurance company."

"I don't know," he says with a shrug. "He just asked me to come help, and I said yes."

"Interesting. Okay, well I haven't seen the kids in a while. I'll give them a snuggle. Sam's getting to that age where he avoids it, but I usually guilt him into giving me a hug."

"The kids love you," Ben says with a grin. "All of the kids do. You're good with them."

"Well, yeah, because I'm the cool aunt." I grin and look down as my phone pings with a text from Gabby.

*The kids have the flu. Probably the same one Ben had. They're quarantined upstairs. Sorry!*

"Well, shit."

"What's wrong?"

"Gabby just texted. The kids have the flu and are not allowed in the common areas. She can't risk spreading the illness to guests." I blow out a gusty breath. "No snuggles for Aunt Van."

"I'll snuggle you," he says and wiggles his eyebrows.

"I've learned a lot about you over the past week," I inform him just as we pull into the driveway of the inn.

"Yeah? What have you learned?"

"I'll tell you later." I move to open my door, but he stops me.

"I'll open your door, Angel."

He's called me that since the night he was sick. I don't know why he uses that specific endearment, but I admit I like it. It's better than *baby* or *honey.*

I'm grinning when he opens my door.

"What?" he says and helps me to my feet, pulling me into his arms for a quick kiss.

"Why do you call me Angel?"

"I'll tell you later," he says, echoing my own words. He shuts the car door, and slaps my ass, lightly, but enough to turn me on and look at him in surprise.

"Well, hello."

"Is that good or bad?"

"That's good, handsome."

"Hey!" Gabby calls from the front door of the inn. She waves and reaches inside for something, then walks out with a picnic basket almost as big as she is.

"Are you going somewhere?" I ask as I climb the steps. She pulls me in for a quick hug.

"Nope. We are," Ben says, relieving her of the basket. His arm flexes as he lifts it, and I immediately want to lick him there.

My hormones are out of control with him. Yet, I'm conflicted. I want to strip him naked, and I'm nervous, all at the same time.

I would guess that's normal.

I hope.

"I thought you were helping Rhys."

"Sugar," Gabby says, patting my shoulder, "Rhys

doesn't need any help. Your man has a surprise for you. Smile and nod."

I do as she says and stare up at Ben. "Okay."

"Okay." He kisses Gabby's cheek just the way he always does when he sees my sisters. "Thanks, Gab. We'll see you in a while."

"No rush. Have fun!"

And with that, she walks away, her hips swaying in the way they do when she's proud of herself, and she disappears inside.

"Okay, where—"

He presses his finger to my lips, sending electricity down my spine.

"No more questions. Just take my hand and walk with me."

Without a word, I link my hand with his, and he leads me down the steps and onto the path that winds around the big house and back toward the rose gardens and the old slave quarters that Gabby renovated so they were safe, and on display for her guests.

"It's a pretty day." I take a deep breath, loving the smell of new flowers. "Spring is my favorite time of year."

"How many summers did we spend out here?" Ben asks as he leads me off of the path and toward my favorite oak tree.

I wonder if he knows it's my favorite tree, or if it's coincidence?

"Well, I spent all of my summers here," I reply with

a grin. "And for as long as I can remember, you were here too."

"At first, my mama would bring me out on the weekends to play with the boys, but finally your mama talked her into letting me just come out here to live with you guys for the summer."

"But your mama still came on the weekends."

"Well, she missed all of us. I don't know why she didn't just come as well. I know she was invited."

"Maybe she had hot, torrid affairs while you were off playing the summer away in the bayou." I glance up to find him frowning down at me. "What?"

"She's my *mother*."

I laugh and rub his arm. "She's a woman, Ben. You can't tell me she's never had a man in her life."

He stops and stares down at me for a moment.

"You've never considered this?"

"No."

"She's a beautiful, lovely person. Of course there must have been men interested in her."

"She never said," he says and shakes his head. "Great, now I'm going to have to have this conversation with her."

"Why?" I can't stop laughing now.

"Because it's going to bug me, and I'll eventually blurt it out anyway."

We turn a corner and there it is, my favorite tree. It's at least four hundred years old, with branches so big and heavy that they rest on the ground.

And under it is a portable swing with a red blanket spread in front of it.

"Oh, my."

He smiles down at me and leads me to the swing. I sit and kick my flip flops off, and Ben sets the basket in the middle of the blanket and joins me on the swing.

"This is lovely."

"It's a good day for it," he says and rests his arm on the back of the swing, behind my shoulders. His fingertips brush the bare skin on my shoulder. I scoot closer to him and rest my head on his shoulder.

"We spent countless summers out here," he says quietly, as if speaking too loud will disrupt the perfect spring day.

"We did."

"And as a teenager, I would see you sitting out here, under this tree, with a book. Your knees pulled up to your chest, and your bare feet dirty as can be. You took my breath away even then."

I glance up at him in surprise.

"I can't tell you how often I'd watch you—not in a creepy way, I might add—I'd watch you reading and enjoying this tree, and I wanted so badly to sit with you and kiss you senseless."

"I didn't know that."

"Of course you didn't," he says with a gentle smile. "But now you do."

He nudges my chin up with his fingers and lowers his lips to mine, covering them softly. I cup his face in

KRISTEN PROBY

my hand and let myself simply soak in this moment, in my favorite place, with this man.

He slowly takes the kiss from sweet to hot, and to my delight, drags his hand from my hip to my breast, his thumb dancing over my already tight nipple.

Good God, he's like a drug that I'll never get tired of.

After what seems like an hour, he pulls back and rests his forehead against mine.

"I have been waiting for that for a very long time," he whispers.

"I think this was probably way better than anything you might have done as a teenager."

He chuckles. "True. So, it's a win-win."

I let my fingertips glide down his cheeks to his neck.

"Savannah."

"Yes?"

"I want you," he says and closes his eyes tightly. "I don't say that to rush you into anything, and this isn't the time or place anyway, but I need you to know that I *want* you."

I cover his lips with mine, watching his eyes. "I want you too, Ben."

He inhales and kisses me again, moving straight into hot as fuck.

Finally, he pulls back, clears his throat, and smiles at me.

"Are you hungry?"

I laugh and push my hair off my face. "So hungry."

"I think Gabby made fried chicken."

"That sounds good too."

He glances at me in surprise and then begins to laugh in earnest. You could cut the sexual chemistry with a knife.

But, he's a perfect gentleman as he opens the basket and we dig in.

The food, and the company, are delicious.

# CHAPTER 8

~SAVANNAH~

"*S*o, quite a bit has happened since I last saw you."

My therapist, Violet, is sitting across from me in her office. When I first started coming here, I thought she'd make me lie down and spill my guts about my whole life, starting with my childhood, but according to her, that's just for movies and TV shows.

I'm sitting in a deep, soft loveseat, and she's across from me on a matching over-sized chair. Violet is also a friend of the family. I don't think I could have told a complete stranger about all of the horrible things that happened when I was married.

"Awesome. Spill it." She grins. Violet is about fifty, with stark-grey hair that she always keeps in a braid. She never wears makeup, and she's thin as a rail. She's also kind and soft spoken, but she can get tough when she needs to.

"I'm officially dating Ben."

Her eyes widen and she makes a note on her legal pad.

"I'm surprised you hadn't heard already."

"I've been on vacation with Lucy in the Bahamas, and we turned our phones off."

"Did you two finally take a honeymoon?"

She smiles like a young girl, her face radiating happiness.

"We did."

"That's awesome. Congratulations again, Violet."

"Thank you." She clears her throat and shifts in the chair. "But let's get back to you. Tell me more about Ben. How did this come about?"

I explain about the day at the hospital, and how he finally shared how he feels, and gave me the choice. I tell her everything, leading up to our amazing day under my favorite tree yesterday.

"Oh, Van, this is wonderful. I'm just ecstatic for you."

"Thank you."

"Have you been intimate?"

I bite my lip and shake my head no. "We've done some fun making out, but no. He hasn't pushed me, and I haven't initiated it, mostly because I don't know how."

"When you think about having sex with Ben, how do you feel?"

"Scared," I whisper and look at Violet with tears in my eyes. "Why am I so afraid of this?"

"Why do *you* think you're afraid?"

"Oh, that's right, I'm talking to my shrink. She doesn't answer questions; she asks them."

Violet smirks and waits patiently for me to answer.

"Well, let's be honest. Lance didn't make sex nice or even comfortable for me. He used sex to terrorize me."

The smile falls from her face and she scribbles on her pad.

"What about men before Lance?"

"I'd only been with two guys before him," I reply and trace the pattern in the couch with my fingertip. "And they were nice, but I was young."

"But those were good experiences?"

"Yes."

"Good." She shifts in the chair again and sets her pad on the table before her. I can see that she wrote *terrorized* and circled it twice. "I don't know if you've ever gone into detail with me about what sex was like with Lance."

I shake my head and look her in the eyes. "No."

"Would you please share that with me now?"

I swallow hard, then take the cap off the water she set out for me and take a long drink. I'm just procrastinating, but I don't care.

Maybe the hour will run out before I have to answer.

I glance at my watch. No such luck.

"In the very beginning, like right after we met and began dating, the sex was good. I'd say *normal* for lack of a better word."

"I understand," she says with a nod, urging me to continue.

"As time progressed, especially after we married, it got rougher. And not in a *oh, this is fun and new* kind of way. I realized that he *liked* to hit me during sex."

"Hard?"

"Sometimes. He never hit me in the face hard enough to give me bruises. But he would slap my face, or my boobs, or my ass. The funny thing is, Ben slapped my butt yesterday, playfully, and I liked it."

She smiles now.

"That's good. It means you trust him, and you know he won't hurt you."

"Ben wouldn't hurt me."

"No, ma'am. Never."

I clear my throat, surprised to feel tears threaten. I've never cried during therapy before.

"So," I continue, trying to distance myself, so it's like I'm just retelling a story that someone else told to me. "He gradually added things like floggers or a whip. He'd only use the whip when I'd misbehaved."

She doesn't say anything, but her face loses all of the happy color she had before.

"He liked to go to these festival-type parties that are put on once a year. People wear costumes, usually sexy ones, and there are displays of different

123

fetishes that you can try out. Like, if you've always wanted to be tied up, a guy will do that to you for fun."

"I've heard of them," Violet says.

"I *hated* going to them, mostly because he'd insist I wear the skimpiest costume that I didn't feel comfortable in, and frankly, I'm more of a traditional girl. The fetish stuff doesn't really interest me."

"Did you tell him that?"

I look at her like she's just suggested I jump off of a bridge. "No."

She nods and I continue.

"It was mostly like that for the majority of our marriage. He would have said he was being a Dominant. But I've read enough to know that a Dominant would never make a submissive do anything against her will."

"You're right. While that community is difficult for some to understand, the core of it is consent."

"I can honestly say that I had little say over my life for the better part of six years."

"Savannah," Violet says and comes to sit next to me for a moment, folding me into a hug.

"Do you do this with all of your clients?"

She chuckles, then lets go and returns to her seat. "No, but I needed that."

"He taught me that sex was control, and pain, and everything horrible."

"And a real man would have shown you that it's the

exact opposite. Being intimate with someone is about affection and connection."

"I wouldn't say that Lance and I were ever intimate," I reply.

"No, you're right." She picks her pad up and writes a few more notes. "Are you worried that the sex would be the same with Ben?"

"Not at all."

"Are you physically attracted to him?"

"Hell, yes." I grin. "I didn't know I could be physically turned on ever again, but he doesn't even have to touch me to turn me on."

"That's wonderful," Violet replies. "It's truly miraculous, Savannah. For many women who have been through the trauma that you have, they never recover enough to have a healthy sex life."

"Well, we haven't had sex yet, so the jury is still out on that."

"Has Ben said anything?"

"He's said he wants me," I reply. "Just yesterday, actually. The chemistry is there. We both feel it. And I want to have sex with him."

"What's holding you back?"

"Well, yesterday he mentioned something about kids, and how good I am with them."

"Okay."

"Do you think that means that he wants kids?"

"What do *you* think it means?"

"Jesus, Violet, will you just answer one question?"

Her lips twitch. "You know Ben better than I do."

I blow out a gusty breath. "I don't know if he wants kids. I would guess so."

"And why does that bother you?"

"Because I can't have children."

She pauses. "Have you always been infertile?"

"No."

"I see. Have you talked to Ben about it?"

"No."

"Well, I think that's where you should start."

"What should I say? And when? Like, we're about to do the deed and I blurt out, *Oh, by the way, if you want kids we need to stop now.*"

"Clearly, that's not the case." She tilts her head to the side. "I know Ben well enough to know that he would listen to you and have an adult conversation with you."

"I know." I sigh. "It's just an awkward conversation, and frankly, I'm sick to death of having to talk about Lance and all the ways he fucked me up. I want it in the past."

"I think opening up to Ben is the best way to put it squarely in your past, Van."

"I've been feeling so much better."

"You are not the same woman who walked into this office two years ago," she confirms. "You're confident and happy. You have yourself back, and that's the result of all of your hard work. I love your hair, by the way."

"Thanks." I run my fingers through the shorter strands of hair. "It was time."

"And maybe it's time for this conversation with Ben as well," she says with a kind smile. "I think you'll be relieved, and his reaction will pleasantly surprise you."

"You think?"

"I do."

I nod and rub my hands on my legs, already nervous. "Probably best to do it sooner, rather than later, right?"

"I agree, yes."

I reach out and take Violet's hand in mine, giving it a squeeze. "Thank you."

"That's what I'm here for."

I JUST KICKED the shit out of someone in Krav Maga class. It was almost as therapeutic as my chat with Violet earlier today. Now I want to go home, take a long hot shower, and curl up with a book by the fire.

I've been with Ben every night since we started this official relationship. Not through the night, aside from the night he was sick. But we have made a point of spending evenings together after work.

I think I should give him a night off from me. I'm always moody after therapy, and I'm tired tonight.

I'm probably not good company.

KRISTEN PROBY

Besides, I need to have *the talk* with him, and I'm avoiding that like the freaking plague.

I hurry home and, after locking myself in, I hurry upstairs to take my shower. Once out, I reach for my perfume on my vanity, but it's gone. I always keep it in the same place, but it's not here.

I glance around in confusion, but I don't see it anywhere.

Huh. Who would have taken it? Surely Ben doesn't need it.

I shrug and mentally add new perfume to my list. I love the scent I use. It's light and pretty, and you have to get close to me to smell it.

Lance used to insist I wear Chanel No. 5, and to this day, if I smell it on someone as they pass by, I get nauseated. I *hate* it.

But I don't have to wear it anymore. I'll pick up another bottle of my fave.

I finish getting dressed and Ben calls.

"Hi there," I say with a smile.

"How are you, beautiful?"

"Tired. It's been a crazy day. How are you?"

"Lonely."

I smirk. "I was thinking about staying home this evening."

"That's fine, I can come there."

I bite my lip. "You don't want a night away from me?"

He's silent for a moment. "Is that what you want?"

I think it over, and it occurs to me that no, that's not what I want.

"I just don't want you to get sick of me."

"Savannah, that's one thing you don't ever have to worry about. Besides I realized that you never spilled the beans about what you've learned about me."

"That's a long list," I say, my inner flirt on full-blast. "I'll come over, if it's okay."

"It's always okay," he says. "Drive carefully."

"I will."

I hang up and gather my things, and am headed to Ben's house within two minutes. My hands are sweaty. My stomach is rolling.

It's a good thing I haven't eaten anything yet. I'd just upchuck it.

"Hey," he says as he swings the door open. "The code to this door is eight-eight-nine-nine."

I cock a brow. "That's pretty simple."

"I like simple," he says with a shrug. As soon as the door is closed, he pulls me in for a tight hug and a long kiss.

"Is it possible to miss you after less than a day?" I ask.

"I guess so," he replies and leads me up to his rec room. He has a big pool table, a big TV, a big wet bar.

Basically, everything is just oversized in this room. If you were to look up *man cave* in the dictionary, this would be there.

"I don't think you've ever brought me up here," I say

and wander around the room, setting my bag on the table behind an enormous sectional couch.

"This is where I usually hang out when I'm home."

He sits on the couch and watches me prowl about.

"You seem tense."

"Me?" I shake my head. "Never."

"Right. Come here." He holds his hand out for mine and I take it, letting him pull me into his lap. "Spill it."

"What?"

"What you've learned."

I kiss his cheek. "I always knew you were kind. But I've learned that you're way more mushy and affectionate than I expected."

"Did you just call me a wuss?" he asks with a frown.

"No." I laugh and kiss his cheek again. "I said you're sensitive."

"Can we keep this our secret?"

"Yes. If other women knew, I'd have to kick their asses to keep them off of you."

"You're the only woman I want."

"See? You say the sweetest things."

He grins and runs his fingers through my hair, making me wish I could purr.

"What else is on your mind?"

I sigh. "I guess I should talk to you about something. This also has to remain a secret between us."

"Okay."

I can't talk about this while in his lap. I just can't. I

stand and pace away from him, trying to decide how to tell him this.

"Are you okay?" he finally asks. "Are you hurt?"

"Not anymore," I murmur. "I guess I can start this with a question for you."

"Shoot." He's still sitting casually, one ankle crossed over the opposite knee, his arm along the back of the couch.

"Do you want children one day?"

His eyes narrow, but he doesn't move otherwise.

"With the right woman, yes." He tilts his head to the side. "Do you?"

"I've always wanted children," I admit. "But I have to tell you, before we take this any further, that I *can't* have kids."

He swallows hard. "Okay. Why?"

I frown.

"You might as well tell me the whole story," he says and stands so he can pick me up and set me on the couch next to him. "And I want you next to me while you do."

"I'm not going to tell you everything." I shake my head when he would argue and take his hand in mine. "Trust me when I tell you, you don't want it all in your head. It's in the past, and I'm so good now, Ben. I can't give him any more power by telling you everything that happened.

"But this part is important because although I know it's still early, it could potentially affect you too, and just like you gave me the freedom to choose this with you, I have to give that back to you."

"Okay, sweetheart. I'm all ears."

I take a deep breath.

"I can't have babies. Ever." I have to pause to find the right words. "I was beaten so severely that he destroyed my ovaries and they had to be removed. I had to have a full hysterectomy."

I risk looking up into his face and what I find there makes me catch my breath.

He has tears in his eyes.

"I don't have to tell you any more."

"Yes, you do." He leans over and kisses me softly. "But only as much as you want."

"Well, that really explains the physiology of it. It wasn't just one beating, but many over the span of a few years that did irreparable damage. My doctor found it during a routine physical, and suggested I had it all removed before it could become infected or worse.

"So, I did." I shrug. "And I needed you to know because if we keep going down this path, and it leads to something permanent later on, you have to know in advance that we could never have children."

"Well, not biological ones anyway. There are plenty of children out there that need a family."

"I've never considered adoption."

"You should," he says. "No matter who you end up with, you should know that that's an option for you.

And as far as I'm concerned, well, I am not willing to walk away from you, Savannah. There's not much you could say to make me go."

A sigh of relief runs through me. "Are you sure?"

"I'm sure." He pulls me back into his lap. "I'm sorry that happened to you, Angel."

"It's over." I pull back and look into his face. "You never told me why you call me Angel."

His lips turn up into a smile.

"Because when I was lying in bed, about to die, you were hovering over me and I could have sworn you were an angel."

"I'm not." I kiss his cheek. "An angel."

"You're as close as I'll ever get to one," he replies. "Do you feel up to a game of pool?"

"I don't know how to play pool."

He stands with me still in his arms.

"I love how strong you are."

"And I love how strong *you* are," he replies. "You're the strongest person I know, Savannah, and it's a privilege to be with you."

"Don't get sappy on me, Mr. Preston."

"Fine. I'll teach you how to play pool instead, Ms. Boudreaux."

I smile, holding onto him and enjoying the feel of his arms around me. "Deal."

# CHAPTER 9

~SAVANNAH~

"*H*old it like this," Ben says. He's pushed up behind me, leaning over me. We're stretched over the table, and let's be honest, I'm not at all focused on getting this green ball in the corner pocket.

I'm focused on Ben's crotch pressed against my ass. His chest pressed to my back.

His lips whispering in my ear.

I've never had sex on a pool table before, and now seems like a great time to start.

I lick my lips and aim for the ball, as Ben guides my arm in slow motions. I strike, and the ball misses, bouncing around the table.

"I don't think you're a great teacher," I say as we both stand up. I already miss the heat of him against me.

"I don't think you're paying attention," he replies,

leaning on the cue, and not backing away. So I boost myself up and sit on the edge of the table, gathering Ben's shirt in my fists at his hips.

"Oh, I'm paying attention." I grin as he lets the cue fall to the tabletop and plants his hands on the table at my hips, leaning in to kiss me.

"Are you really in the mood to play pool?" he asks against my lips.

"I don't think so." I tug his shirt up and let my hands explore his warm, smooth skin.

"Angel, I need to be sure that *you're* sure about this," he says, holding my face in his hands and pinning me in his ice-blue stare.

"I'm sure."

"I'm going to take this *very* slowly."

"Because you're trying to torture me?" I grin and bite his lip.

"No, smart ass, because I've dreamed about this for years, and because I want to make sure that you feel safe."

"I've never felt safer in my life than I do when I'm with you, Ben." I take his hand and place it over my heart. "I love you. I trust you implicitly, and I *want* you."

His eyes close as if in relief for a millisecond, and the next thing I know, he's lifted me and is carrying me toward the bedroom.

"No pool table sex?"

He stops cold and stares at me in surprise. "Do you *want* to have pool table sex?"

"Well, it sounds like it could be fun."

He laughs and carries me the rest of the way to his bedroom.

"Then pool table sex we shall have, beautiful lady. But not this time. This time, I want you in my bed. I want your scent on my sheets. I want to see the moonlight on your gorgeous skin as we lie here and worship each other."

"Wow. I had no idea you were a poet." I smile sweetly, but then he shocks the hell out of me and whips his shirt right over his head. "God, Ben, you're just ridiculous."

His lips twitch. "Now it's your turn." He grabs the hem of my shirt and lifts it slowly. I raise my arms over my head and when it's off, he lets it fall to the floor. His eyes are still pinned to mine, and then they very deliberately travel down my neck, to my chest and my stomach. "Beautiful."

*You haven't seen the stomach pooch yet.*

But I don't say it out loud because no man wants his girl to start talking shit about herself when they're about to make love. It's not sexy at all.

I reach out to unfasten his jeans. He watches me patiently, his hands hanging at his sides, as I pull them down his hips and legs. I crouch next to him, helping him step out of them. Before I stand back up, I take my time kissing his strong thighs. He has a light dusting of hair that feels good against my lips.

He's just in his tight boxer briefs now. They're

black, and they cling in the most delicious way. He's clearly aroused, so I lean in and press a kiss over the cotton of his shorts.

"Oh no," he says, guiding me back to my feet. "You have to catch up."

"You catch me up," I reply, making him smile. His fingers make quick work of my jeans, and he copies my move of squatting before me, tugging them down my legs. I brace myself on his shoulder as I step out of them.

And then, praise the Lord above, he presses a kiss to my thigh, mirroring my movements.

Holy shit, he's going to kiss me *there*.

And he does. His lips are firm as he kisses me over my pink cotton panties, and then he stands again, gazing happily down at me.

We're standing here, in our underwear, just staring at each other. It might be the most intimate moment of my life.

"You're perfect," he whispers. He reaches out to trace my bra strap down to the top of the cup. "Every part of me wants to take you fast and hard, but I must admit, this is amazing."

I nod and step closer to him, pressing my belly against his hard on.

"You didn't get your tattoo," he says.

"Not yet. You got sick, so I postponed."

He kisses my forehead.

"I need to tell you," he says, as his hands travel over

my skin, sending zings of electricity all over me. It's hard to keep my eyes open. I feel drunk.

And he's just getting started.

Dear, sweet Jesus, I might not survive this.

"What do you need to tell me?" I whisper.

"You're amazing, Savannah." He presses his lips ever so gently to the soft skin below my ear. "You're the most fantastic person I've ever known in my life, and I love you so much my body aches with it."

"Ben," I whisper, completely mesmerized by him.

His hands glide up my arms, over my shoulders, and to my back where he unfastens my bra and I let it fall down my arms and to the floor.

My nipples are already hard pebbles. I have goose bumps all over my skin. His breath, his eyes, his fingers are seducing me faster than anything else ever has.

I'm already addicted to him, and we've hardly touched each other.

"Beautiful," he says again and presses a kiss on my chest, right between my breasts.

"You're not naked yet," I say. I'm tracing the very top of his boxer briefs, where the elastic meets his skin.

"Neither are you," he replies and I smile up at him.

"You first."

He cocks his head to the side and holds his arms out. "Help yourself."

He's making sure I know that I'm in control, and it's just as touching as him declaring his love for me.

I slip my finger under the elastic, never looking

away from his face. I can feel his smooth skin, pulled tight over his erection. The ridge of the head leads me to the very tip, and...*metal?*

"Um, Ben?"

"Yes, Angel."

"Are you pierced?"

His lips tip up into a smile. "I am."

I'm fascinated.

"I have to see this." I pull his shorts down, freeing his cock, and stare in wonder not only at the metal ring he's sporting in the tip, but the sheer size of him.

"That will not fit inside me."

He chuckles. "I promise, it will."

"I'm going to have so many questions for you later."

"I hope so," he says as I push the shorts down around his ankles. He steps free of them, and here he is, in all of his glory.

And let me just say, he's mother fucking glorious.

"Can you please turn around?" I ask and bite my lip. He doesn't ask why, or argue at all. He simply turns his back to me.

I knew I loved his tattoos. His sleeves are impressive. The others on his torso are beautiful.

But I had no idea that I could be this turned on by someone's *back.*

The muscles are defined, rippled under inked skin. He doesn't have his whole back covered, just up between his shoulder blades.

"What does the symbol on your back mean?"

"It's the Krav Maga symbol," he replies. He's being so patient with me, letting me take my time to look him over.

His ass is firm, and he has those two dimples right above it.

I reach out and trace one, then the other.

"You can turn back around," I say and smile at him when he complies. "I don't want you to get a big head or anything, but you are physically ridiculous."

"Thank you," he says. "Now, it's my turn."

I hold my arms out at my side and smirk, mirroring his response from a minute ago. He steps to me and brushes his finger over the elastic, where it meets the skin along my waist.

I'm so damn wet right now, the panties will be soaked when he finally gets them off of me.

"I'm going to take these off," he whispers.

"Great." He hooks his thumbs in the waistband at my hips and slowly drags them down my legs, kissing my exposed skin and sending more goosebumps over my body. When they're pooled at my feet, he stands and steps back so he can take a good, long look. I don't even care that he's looking at my belly, given the pure lust in his eyes. "Please turn around."

I comply and hear him suck in a breath. I know I have a couple of scars on my back. They're not as bad as they could be, and I don't have to see them, so I forget they're there.

Well, most of the time.

"Lift your hair off your neck, please."

I grin and do as he asks.

"What does that one mean?" He's referring to the tattoo just under my hairline.

"It's a lotus flower. They rise out of the mud and are beautiful. I got it in college. It seemed pretty and symbolic, and had no idea just *how* symbolic it would end up being."

"I agree," he says. "You can let your hair down and turn around."

He steps to me and cups my chin and neck in his palm. "I'm going to take my time tonight, Van. I want to explore you. I want to learn you."

"Same page," I whisper.

He urges me onto the bed, finally. The covers are cool against my already hot skin. He climbs on with me, covering me completely. His erection is heavy on my belly, and I love it. I can't help myself, I reach down and cup him in my hand and watch with satisfaction as he closes his eyes and curses under his breath.

"If you keep doing that, it won't be slow, sweetheart."

I love that I'm turning him on as much as he is me. I love that there's just the two of us here, no ghosts from the past. Just us, and this incredible attraction for each other.

I let go of him as he begins to pepper kisses over my neck. He kisses, then licks, and then moves on to the next spot, bless his heart.

"I thought the whole V in the hips thing was something reserved only for romance novels," I whisper as he travels down my chest. He licks my navel, and I have to bite my lip to keep from laughing.

It tickles.

I'm shocked that I feel so comfortable here, naked, with the one man I've wanted for as long as I can remember.

"You have a beautiful body." He licks his way over to my hip and then up my side.

"Are you going to do this over my *entire* body?"

He stops and looks up at me. "Do you have something against this?"

"No." I shake my head and brush his hair off his forehead. "It's nice. But I'm not doing anything for you."

"You'll have the chance to repay the favor." And with that, he goes back to exploring every inch of my body. Every nerve ending is quivering as he touches, kisses, licks, and bites his way all over me.

He flips me over on my stomach and starts at my feet, making his way up. He plants a wet kiss on both ass cheeks, making me giggle.

"Your stubble feels so good."

"I should have shaved," he says.

"I like it."

"Yes, but I plan to kiss you here." His fingers slide up between my legs and into my folds, and we both moan in pleasure. "You're so fucking wet, Angel."

"In case you missed it, I'm incredibly turned on."

"I haven't missed a thing," he murmurs. His fingers have moved on, abandoning my core completely. I want to pout, but then he sucks on the small of my back.

Jesus, who knew the small of my back was a fucking erogenous zone?

"Like that?"

"Mm." I can't speak now as he nibbles his way up my spine.

"You have scars." He traces one with his tongue.

"They're fading."

"I have some lotion I'll put on them later." He bites my shoulder. "It'll help."

"Oh my God." I have to hang on for dear life as he kisses my lotus flower. My hips buck, my nipples are pebbles, and I've never come so close to orgasm from foreplay in my life.

"Good or bad?"

"Don't stop. If you stop, I'll have to beat you up."

He chuckles and repeats the motion.

"You're finding all kinds of erogenous zones I didn't know existed."

"That's my job." He flips me over again, and I'm staring up into the bluest eyes that rival the ocean. "By the time we're finished, I don't want you to remember your name."

"I definitely couldn't spell it right now."

His hand glides down my side to my hip. His cock is

143

pressed to my thigh, and he's kissing me now, like he's starving.

Finally, *finally,* he urges my legs apart. He doesn't leave my lips as his fingers brush ever so lightly over my pussy. I'm so aroused, that all it takes is that gentle touch to have my hips rise up off the bed, seeking him out.

"Ben," I gasp, holding on for dear life.

"What do you need?"

"You." I'm riding his fingers now. I couldn't stop if I wanted to, and I certainly don't want to. "I need you."

He positions himself between my legs, wrapping them around his hips.

"Watch," he says. I glance down and watch as the head of his cock, and that piece of metal, slips through my folds and inside me in the slowest, smoothest motion. When he's in all the way, he stops and kisses me softly, and I can't help the tear that falls from the corner of my eye. "Are you okay, love?"

"I'm so okay," I reply. "You feel *so good*, and I'm happy to be here with you. It's so much more amazing than I ever thought it could be."

He rests his forehead on mine and begins to move in slow, shallow thrusts, allowing my body to adjust to him.

"You're so tight," he whispers.

"It's been a *very* long time." I bite my lip, wishing I hadn't said that. What an idiot! But Ben being the kind man he is, he kisses me and grins.

"For me too," he informs me, defusing what could have been an awkward moment. "My God, Van, this is better than anything in my dreams."

"You can move faster."

He cocks a brow. "Yes, ma'am." His hips move faster, and he's pushing a bit harder, and I can feel that little piece of metal hitting just the right spot, over and over again.

"Holy shit."

"There you go," he croons, watching my face. "That's it, Savannah. Just ride the wave."

I'm helpless to do anything but, as he reaches under me and tips my hips up, and that's all it takes to make me explode into a million tiny pieces.

He buries his face in my neck and groans.

"You're squeezing me so hard."

His words have me squeezing even harder, and his whole body tightens, and he comes apart, giving in to his own orgasm.

I hold him tightly as he recovers, brushing his hair off of his forehead, letting my other hand roam down his side to his impressive ass and up his back again.

After he catches his breath, he carefully pulls out and collapses next to me. He still has enough energy to pull me to him, tucking me safely against him.

"None of this should surprise me," I say, my fingers brushing up and down his arm.

"What's that?"

"The chemistry. The trust. The love. How comfortable I am with you."

"Those are all excellent things."

"I didn't think I'd ever feel them again," I admit and roll in his arms so I'm facing him. I cup his cheek in my hand and lay my lips against his gently. "It feels...*so damn good.* Ben, being with you these past couple of weeks has done just as much good for me as two years of therapy."

"I should put that on a T-shirt. It would be great for business."

I laugh and kiss his chin. "Thank you, just for being you."

"I'm just trying to be as honest and careful with you as I can be. Not because you're fragile. You're not. But because I don't want to fuck this up, Savannah. We worked too hard to get here."

"We're not going to fuck it up." I tuck my face in his neck and breathe him in. "I heard a saying once. *His love roars louder than her demons.* I can't explain this any better than that."

He kisses the crown of my head. He's brushing my hair back, sifting it through his fingers, over and over again. It feels so *good.*

"Tell me about the piercing."

He shifts, wrapping one leg around mine and clears his throat.

"Are you sure you want this story?"

"Oh, I'm riveted."

"It might make you run and never come back."

I frown and look up into his eyes and see that he's being playful. He's smirking; his eyes are full of fun.

I slap his ass and tuck myself against him again.

"Spill it, Benjamin."

## CHAPTER 10

~BEN~

*T*his, right here, is everything I've ever wanted in my life. She fits perfectly in every way. Her body is absolutely every fantasy I've had, but more than that, we fit together like this, curled up together, like two pieces of a puzzle.

I kiss her head, and keep playing with her hair, tickling the back of her neck where her sexy little tattoo is, and I can tell by her sweet little moans that it feels good.

"I was young," I begin, not exactly excited to tell this story. "And in college."

"It's amazing how many stories begin with that." She snorts and traces the muscles in my upper arms, along with the tattoos there. Ironically, the one she's tracing right now is her tattoo.

"Someone should put a book together of stories that start that way," I reply.

"I'm sure it's already been written."

"Hm." I kiss her lips when she tips her head back.

"Okay, keep going."

"Okay, so I was young and stupid, and I can't confirm or deny, but I might have also been drunk."

"So you were drunk…"

I laugh and keep going. "I'd already started my right sleeve, so I went in to this tattoo and piercing place pretty regularly, and there was this girl."

"The other way most stories start."

"Yes. But I have to say, if you're uncomfortable—"

"Please." She rolls her eyes. "You're no virgin, Ben. Keep talking."

"So, this girl was the piercer at the tattoo shop, and the guy who did my tats set me up with her. She was nice enough, not much drama, pretty fun to hang out with."

"How long did you date her?"

"Oh, maybe three months?" I shrug. "Not long because she eventually talked me into getting the piercing."

"And is this a Prince Albert or an Apa?" she asks, and I have to stop and stare at her.

"How do you know the names of these?"

"Um, I'm not dumb," she says and slaps my arm. "And I went to college, too."

"Right." *I don't want to think about that.* "This is a Prince Albert. And we stopped dating because once

149

this happened, I was sore for about six months. She didn't warn me that that was a side effect."

"I always thought it was an urban myth that the piercing did anything for the girl during sex, but I can now attest that it's true."

"Really?" Now I'm fascinated. I push her onto her back so I have better access to the rest of her body. "How so?"

"Well, it definitely brushed against the other urban myth several times."

"Your G spot?"

"Oh yeah," she says, nodding vigorously. "Definitely found that sweet little spot."

"Huh." I rub her belly, tracing circles around her navel. "I know how to find that spot without the metal."

"I doubt it."

I cock a brow. "You don't believe me?"

She shrugs one shoulder as if it's no big deal. "Most men think they know how to find it, and most definitely don't."

"Shall we bet on it?"

"What would you like to bet?"

She's smiling so widely, her hazel eyes shining with humor and lust, and it's all I can do not to pin her down and fuck her mindless.

"The loser has to order pizza and get dressed to get it when it arrives."

She moves her head from side to side, as if she's thinking it over, and finally nods. "Deal."

*Oh, sweetheart, you're about to lose this bet.*

I kiss her pubis and urge her legs apart. She readily complies and when I position myself between her thighs and glance up at her, she's staring down at me with pure lust and hunger.

I kiss the crease of her leg and her pussy and she grins. "That's not it."

"Ha ha."

I push two fingers inside her and make a *come here* motion that sends her head back on the pillow, thrashing back and forth.

"Holy shit!"

I grin and keep going, adding my thumb to her clit, and watch in fascination as she comes hard. She reaches above her to push on the headboard as her cheeks and neck flush. When I feel the last spasms, I pull my fingers out and smile up at her.

"I want sausage on my pizza."

"How do you know it worked?"

I can't help it, I stop and stare at her for a second and then bust up laughing, pulling her to me.

"You crack me up."

"I guess it's a win-win for me," she says. "I just had another orgasm *and* I get pizza."

"That's a great way of looking at it."

"Are you hungry now?" She's searching for something, frowning.

"What's wrong?"

"I can't find my phone."

"It's probably still in the pool room. I'll go get it."

I dash down the hall and find the pool room just as we left it, the lights still on, balls scattered on the table. Her handbag is in the couch, so I just grab the whole thing and bring it back to her. She's sitting on the side of the bed, her clothes already back on.

"Oh, thanks."

"You got dressed."

"Well, yeah. I have to order pizza and get it from the delivery guy. I don't think you want me answering the door in my birthday suit."

"No, but I wasn't ready for you to get dressed yet either."

"Don't sulk," she says as she pulls her phone out of her bag. She frowns when she looks down. "Beau's been blowing up my phone."

"Go ahead and call him."

She nods and presses the phone to her ear. It doesn't take him long to answer.

"Hey, what's up?" She's silent as she listens, and then her eyes widen and she smiles happily. "Really? She is? Oh my God, Beau." Her eyes fill with tears and she sniffles. "Of course I'm crying. No, they're happy tears. Oh, I'm so happy for you. Please hug her for me, and tell her I want to see her tomorrow. Okay. Good night."

"Well?"

"Did he blow up your phone too?"

"I don't have any idea where my phone is," I reply. "I've had other things on my mind."

"Well, Mallory is going to have a baby." She pulls a tissue out of her bag and blows her nose. Jesus, what else do women carry in those things?

"That's awesome."

"I know." And now she breaks down in tears again. "She's always been afraid to have kids because the girls in her family inherit her paranormal abilities, but Beau is so good for her, and I'm so h-h-happy for them."

"I see that." I tug her hand and pull her up into my arms, rocking us both back and forth. I wonder if she's torn when one of her siblings says they're going to have a baby. Is she happy for them and sad for herself at the same time?

I don't want to ask her that now. I don't want any ghosts here tonight. So I kiss her temple and wipe the tears away.

"We'll congratulate them tomorrow."

She nods, the tears drying up.

"Are you hungry?" I ask.

"Yes."

"Let's order that pizza then."

"TODAY WAS A KICK-MY-ASS DAY," Ethan, my general manager, says the following evening as we're closing up the studio.

"Anything you need help with?" I ask him.

153

"No, nothing crazy, just busy. I had two women come in together today and join Shelly's class."

"That's great." I started that class right after we all discovered just how badly Savannah's ex-husband abused her. "We might have to add another of her classes each week. It's pretty full."

"It's great for us, but it's fucking sad that there are that many women who need to defend themselves against men who are supposed to love them."

"And that's just the ones who have discovered the class and are brave enough to come," I reply.

"I know." He sighs. "I have some more paperwork to catch up on, but I'll be right behind you."

"I can stay."

"No, I'll literally be thirty seconds behind you. I'll lock up on my way out."

"All right, man, have a good night."

He waves me off and I snag my keys off my desk. It's after dark, but that's not unusual on Thursdays when I work late. I don't expect my staff to always take the evening classes, and I don't mind doing them, so I teach late on Thursdays.

I walk out of the door and take two steps toward my car when I'm suddenly grabbed on both sides.

"What the fuck?"

I spin, almost freeing myself, but two more men join them. They're massive, outweighing me by at least fifty pounds each.

"Take my wallet," I say, hoping one of them loosens

his grip on me long enough to grab for it, but no such luck.

Thug number three punches me, square in the mouth, cutting it open.

I kick up, using the first two as leverage, but they grab my legs. Thank God I'm fast and I pull back before they can plant their elbow in my shin, breaking it.

"Hey!" I hear Ethan yell and they immediately drop me, but just before they let go completely, Thug One mutters in my ear.

"Stay away from her."

And then I'm lying on the street and the four of them are running away.

"What the fuck?" Ethan asks as he helps me to my feet.

"That's what I said." I dab my lip. It's bleeding.

"They're wearing masks," he says as we watch them disappear into the night.

"And they didn't say much," I reply. "Let's go back in so I can grab a towel. I'm not going straight home from here."

"No problem." He picks my keys up from the side-walk. "Did they mug you?"

"No." I follow him into the studio. "I told them to take my wallet, hoping they'd loosen their grip on me, but they didn't take it."

He narrows his eyes.

"I think it was one of our girls' ex-husband. He said,

*stay away from her."*

"Assholes," Ethan mutters. "Are you okay?"

"Yeah, the lip is the worst of it." I shake my head and toss the bloodied towel in the hamper. "I'm gonna go get a drink with my friends. Would you like to join us?"

"Nah, my wife has dinner waiting." He smiles. "We need security cameras outside, now that we have the girls coming here. Obviously their exes are pissed."

"Of course they are. The women they got off on hurting can hurt them back now." I nod and hold the door for Ethan, then lock it behind us. "And you're right. I'll make some calls tomorrow."

We're parked near each other, and soon Ethan waves as he gets in his car and heads home to his wife.

I'm going to The Odyssey, the bar Declan and his wife co-own, to meet up with the guys. It's in the Quarter, which is hopping tonight. Spring always brings more tourists to New Orleans. I park about a block away from the restaurant.

"Hey," Eli calls out, catching my attention. They're all gathered around the bar.

They're *all* here, which is rare these days with everyone busy with their own lives. Declan is behind the bar with his friend, and the other co-owner of the bar, Adam. Beau, Eli, Rhys, and Simon are sitting on stools, nursing beers and flipping each other shit.

That's what we do.

"You're late," Rhys says, then frowns when he sees my face. "Who gave you the fat lip?"

This attracts all of their attention, but I wave it off. "It's not a big deal."

"Here's some ice," Adam says. "What does the other guy look like?"

"There were four of them," I reply, starting to feel sore where the fuckers grabbed me, and my lip is swelling like a son of a bitch. "Jumped me outside of work."

"Jesus, Ben," Beau says with a frown. "Mugging?"

"No, I think it's one of the students in Shelly's class's ex." I shrug and take a sip of cold beer. "I'm going to have to beef up security outside."

"How do you know that's what it was?" Simon asks.

"One of them told me to *stay away from her.*"

I take another sip, thinking it all over. "You guys don't think it could have been related to Lance, do you?"

They all frown and Eli shakes his head no. "He's in prison. And no one here is going to help him."

"He's in maximum security," Beau adds. "I sincerely doubt it has anything to do with Savannah. What you suggest makes the most sense."

"You're right."

"I never thought I'd see the day that Ben got his ass kicked," Adam says with a smile.

"Oh, you should have seen him last week," Eli says. "Savannah gave him a shiner."

"Shut up," I reply, glaring at my so-called friend.

"This is not good advertising for your business,"

Simon says, joining in on their fun. He's the newest man to join our fold, marrying Charly about a year ago.

"Sure it is," Rhys says, slapping me on the back. "He's a walking billboard for why people *need* to take his class."

They all laugh, and I join in. It's ridiculous. I haven't taken this many shots without giving it back ten-fold in years.

I'll be working out extra hard this week.

"Congratulations, man," I say to Beau and lean in for a man-hug. "Was this a surprise?"

"Yes and no," he says with a shrug. "We decided that we would like to have kids, so we threw birth control out the window, and she got pregnant the first month."

"Over-achievers," Rhys says with a grin.

"Are you having more babies?" Declan asks Rhys who shakes his head.

"No, we're happy with the two we have. I got snipped last year."

We all stare at him in horror.

"It's far easier for me to take care of it than for her, so why not? I protect her. That's what I fucking do."

"Good man," Simon says with a nod.

"What about you guys?" Eli asks.

"Charly and I don't want children," he replies with a shrug. "And you're all reproducing enough for us to spoil and love them. Changing nappies isn't really my forte."

"I don't think changing nappies is any of our forte," Eli says. "But I sure change my fair share."

"Are we really talking about babies in a bar?" Declan asks. "Here, let's do a shot. We're grown men for Christ's sake."

We laugh, and I pass on the shot. One beer is plenty for me.

"So, what exactly are the girls doing over at Van's place?"

"Another séance," Beau says with a sigh. "But Mallory said there aren't any spirits in Van's house, so I'm pretty sure it was just an excuse to get together."

"Gabby said they also wanted to start planning for Mallory's baby shower," Rhys adds.

"Again with the baby talk," Eli says, rolling his eyes.

"I want to know how things are going between Van and Ben," Declan says, watching me closely.

"They're fine," I reply, intending to leave it at that.

"You're going to have to say more than that," Simon replies.

I sigh and glance around at these men who are brothers to me and can't help but chuckle.

"How do I navigate this?" I ponder out loud. "I mean, you're my best friends, but you're also her *brothers.* I can't win here."

"Tonight we're friends," Declan says. "Unless you say something we don't like."

"Exactly," I reply and laugh, then scowl because it made my lip hurt.

Fuckers.

"I don't know what you guys want to know. Let's start with that."

"I want to know if you've started having sex," Adam says and then laughs when the others glare at him. "What? She's not my sister."

"We can kill you and make it look like an accident," Eli informs him, but Adam isn't bullied in the least. He just laughs again and walks down the bar to help a customer.

"Seriously, this is the part that made Van and I think that we shouldn't be together."

"Fuck that," Beau says with a scowl. "We love you both. If it doesn't work out, we still love you both."

"After we beat you up," Declan adds.

"You can try," I reply.

"Obviously it's not hard; just look at your face," Rhys adds, earning a glare from me.

"Okay, I'll just say it all at once, like tearing off a Band Aid." I clear my throat and stare at my beer glass. "I'm in love with her. She's the most amazing woman I've ever known, and she's finally mine. I'm not going to do anything to fuck that up. Yes, we're intimate, and yes, we had a few discussions to make sure she was ready, and that she trusts me."

"So you're not pushing her too hard," Declan says.

"No, but what you all need to remember is, your sister isn't made of glass. My God, she survived something that would have destroyed a lesser person. She's not fragile. And she's done a kick ass job of healing herself."

"You're right," Beau says. "She's not fragile. But she's ours, so we are going to ask these questions, especially given what she *did* live through."

"You know that she's a different person than she was," I reply, looking my best friend square in the eyes. "She's...*Savannah*. She smiles and laughs easily, she's confident in herself. She's happy. And I like to think that I have a hand in that."

"You do," Eli replies. "She and I spoke, and you are an important part of her happiness these days."

"You look good together," Simon says. "I know I'm new around here, but when I first met her, Savannah was still sorting it all out. I'd say she has it sorted."

"And it's about fucking time that she's happy," Rhys says.

"Jesus, we've told you for months to make a move," Beau reminds me. "I'm glad you finally took our advice."

"That's not what I did." I shake my head. "I just couldn't handle it anymore. Being near her, but not *with* her. Can any of you imagine the torture of that? Being a part of your woman's life, but not having her as your woman?"

"No," Rhys says, shaking his head. "I can't imagine it."

"I love her," I say again. "And I'll protect her and love her for the rest of my life."

"I don't think I've ever seen Ben quite this sentimental," Simon says with a grin. "Good for you, mate."

I shrug. "Despite the cut lip, and all the feelings, I'm still badass."

"Of course," Eli says. "We'll see just how badass in the gym tomorrow."

"I'm going to kick your ass."

# CHAPTER 11

## ~SAVANNAH~

"**W**hat's the biggest lie you've ever told?" My sister-in-law, Callie, asks me. We're sitting in my living room, sipping wine with Kate while the others are gathered in my dining room having their tarot cards read by Mallory's best friend, Lena.

Kate thinks about it for a while and then shrugs. "I try not to lie. What about you, Van?"

"I'm okay," I reply and offer them both a smile. "I used to say *I'm okay* a lot. I wasn't okay."

"I hope you plan to never say that again if it isn't true," Callie says, swirling her wine in her glass.

"I don't have a reason to lie these days." I smile as the importance of that statement begins to really sink in. "And that's a pretty cool thing."

"Coolest thing I've ever heard," Kate says with a nod. "I'm happy for you. I was worried for you for a long time, and then I was relieved that you were able to get away from that jackass motherfucker forever, but now that I can see how at peace you are, I just couldn't be happier."

"Don't make me cry," I say, pointing at her. "I don't want to cry this expensive mascara off."

"Okay." She holds her hands up in surrender. "I'm not going to say any more, except atta girl."

"Oh my gosh, you guys," Gabby says as she rushes into the room. "You'll never guess what Lena just told me."

"That you're going to win the lottery?" I ask, unable to keep from laughing when Gabby glares at me, sighing because I've just stolen her thunder.

"Funny. No, she said that I'm going to embark on a new journey."

"Did she use the word *embark?*" Kate asks and smirks into her wine glass.

"You guys are no fun," Gabby replies and stomps back into the dining room, her shoulders sagging in defeat.

"I just like to flip her shit," I say to Callie and Kate. "It's pretty much my only job as a sister. This was fun. It's been too long since we all hung out."

"I had a great time," Mallory says as she joins us. She flops into a chair, looking pleasantly exhausted. She's already started glowing with her pregnancy. Her violet eyes are shining with happiness, and the small smile on her lips gives her the *I have an awesome secret* tilt to it.

Except, it's no secret. And it's more than awesome.

"How have you been feeling?" Kate asks.

"Not horrible," she says. "I mean, I have moments of nausea, and I'm quite sure someone keeps punching my boobs because they hurt like crazy, but otherwise, I feel healthy."

"I have to ask," I say and bite my lip.

"You can ask whatever you like," she says, and I can see that she means it, so I dive in.

"I'm just wondering, since you're psychic, can you already tell the sex of the baby?"

She smiles softly and lays her hand over her belly. "Actually, yes, which is surprising because I can't see the future. I haven't told Beau that yet. I knew I was pregnant before I took a test."

"You need to tell him, so you can tell us," Callie says. "Because I don't know if you've heard, but the Boudreaux women like to buy baby stuff. It's a good thing you and Beau have that huge new house to accommodate it all."

Mallory tucks her long dark hair behind her ear. She recently colored it again.

"I love the new color," I tell her.

"It's actually my natural color. Since I can't have my roots touched up while I'm pregnant I figured I'd go back to my natural color for a while."

"I like it," I say again.

"How are you and Ben doing?" Callie asks and all eyes turn to me.

"Hey!" Gabby calls to us. "We all need to be in on that conversation!"

"Well, then get your butts in here," Kate calls back. Within minutes, Gabby, Charly, and Lena join us in the living room. Some share the couch, others sit on the floor.

It feels like a birthday party sleepover from when I was a teenager.

Except we have wine now, so there's that.

"Okay," Gabby says as she wiggles her bottom, getting comfortable on the floor. "Spill it."

"Ben and I are good." I leave it at that and take a sip of my wine.

"And?" Mallory says.

"Have you said the *I love you*s yet?" Charly asks.

"Yes."

"WHAT?" Gabby exclaims, her eyes wide in horror. "And you didn't call me?"

"Well, it was right before we were about to make love, and I didn't think it was polite to ask him to hold on while I made a slew of phone calls."

"That's fair," Kate says with a nod. "Keep going."

"So not fair," Gabby whispers.

"Yeah, keep going," Callie adds. "How was the sex?"

"Come on, guys. It's Ben. How do you *think* the sex is?"

"She has a point," Mallory says with a nod.

"Seriously, Ben is hot," Lena agrees. "Don't worry, I

understand he's all yours, but I'm sorry, I'm a woman. I have seen him."

"Don't be sorry," I reply, waving her off. "The man is ridiculously perfect physically."

"As long as you don't think he's *perfect* perfect," Charly says.

"He's a human being, just like me, and he's far from perfect. But he's perfect for *me*." I clear my throat, suddenly feeling emotional, which, despite feeling near the edge of tears over the past couple of weeks, is new to me. It's been a long time since I let anything affect me to the point of tears, and I don't know why I'm suddenly so weepy now. "I guess that I didn't know how bad it was before until I discovered how good it can be, you know?"

"I totally understand," Kate says with a nod and tears of her own.

"I know you do," I reply and reach over to squeeze her hand. "And I feel stupid, like I should have known Ben was the one for me all along."

"He wasn't the one for you yet," Mallory says quietly. "People fit differently in our lives at different times. You weren't meant to be with him until now, because you weren't the person you are until now."

"I believe that," I say slowly. "And I wonder if we'd dated a decade ago, if it would have stuck. We were both young, and like Mallory said, different people. The chemistry was always there, at least on my part. From what he's told me, he felt it then, too. But would we have really fallen in love? I'm not so sure. And if we *had* fallen in love, the odds of it surviving through college are probably smaller."

"I'm so happy for you," Charly says and dabs at her eyes. "Watching what you went through was the greatest torture of my life."

"I think it's safe to say we all felt that way," Gabby says and the others nod.

"Even though I didn't meet you until after it all happened," Callie says, "I knew that you'd been to hell and back. No one deserves that."

"But everyone deserves to have an amazing person in their life," Lena says and then smiles ruefully. "And now that I have Mason in my life, I actually believe it."

"I told you that you wouldn't be single forever," Mal says, smiling at her friend.

"The important thing," Lena says with a roll of the eyes, "is that Savannah is happy and safe."

"Very happy and safe," I reply with a satisfied grin. "And well sexed. I shouldn't tell you guys this—"

"Now you *have* to tell," Callie says.

"Absolutely. This is the cone of silence." This is from Gabby, who nods solemnly.

"She's cut off," Callie says with a laugh.

"Seriously, talk," Charly says.

"So, Ben has a piercing."

There's silence for a moment while they all stare at me, and then Callie gasps.

"No!"

"Yes."

"What kind of piercing?" Kate asks, not catching on. "Certainly not his ears or his face. That's not Ben's style."

"You're right. Not on his face. He has a Prince Albert," I blurt and then cover my mouth as if I can't believe I just told them. But these are my *sisters*. I tell them everything.

"Holy shit," Lena says.

"Does it do what they say?" Callie asks.

"Oh yeah."

"Lucky bitch," Charly says, but then shrugs it off. "Who am I kidding? Simon may not have his dick pierced, but he's fucking amazing in the sack."

"I'm so relieved to hear that, darling," the man himself says as he walks into the room, followed by all of my brothers and Ben.

Ben, who is currently staring at me in disbelief.

"Oh, lord."

"You told them?" he asks in disbelief.

"Well, I mean, maybe. But I didn't tell them anything specific about the sex itself."

"I think I'd rather you told them that," he says and picks me up out of my seat, sits down and settles me in his lap while everyone looks on with a mixture of shock and swoon. "Hi, Angel."

"Hi."

"Which one of these assholes bloodied your lip?" I ask, immediately concerned at the cut on his lip, and the bruise along his jaw. "I'll kick their ass and defend your honor."

"No need," he says and kisses my shoulder. "None of them did this. They can't take me."

"Standing right here, man," Eli says with a smirk.

"I'll tell you about it later," Ben adds. "Did you miss me?"

"Yes."

"Oh, sweet baby Jesus," Charly mutters. "They're in full-on mush mode."

"You're mushy," Callie says to her. "Ever since you met Simon, your face goes all gooey when he walks in a room."

"Is that true?" Simon asks Charly and pulls her to her feet so he can plant the kiss of the century on her.

"Well, maybe," she admits. "Let's go home."

"Let's. I have to remind you that I'm fucking amazing in the sack, despite my lack of metal."

She waves as they leave. Over the next fifteen minutes, the rest of them leave, giving Mallory and Beau extra hugs of congratulations.

"You're next," Gabby says to me with a wink, but I just shrug. I tell my sisters everything, but I haven't been strong enough to tell them *that*.

Mallory hugs me and pauses as her arms close around me. Finally, she whispers in my ear, "Some children are born from the heart, not the body. Remember that."

I have to bite my lip to keep from crying as she steps away and lets Beau lead her out of the house.

When everyone is gone, I sit on the couch with a long, gusty sigh. "I love them all so much it hurts. But dear Moses, that's a lot of strong personality in one room."

"I'm always exhausted after family gatherings," Ben says.

"Come sit with me and tell me what happened to your face." I pat the seat next to mine, and he complies, pulling me against him and kissing my temple.

"It was just a weird mugging outside of the studio."

"A what?" I frown up at him and can't resist reaching up to touch the cut on his lip. "That looks painful."

"It *is* a bit painful," he admits. "I don't know who they were. They didn't try to mug me, they just wanted to beat me up. Got a few swings in before Ethan came outside and then they ran. I think it was plotted by an ex of one of the girls in Shelly's class."

I frown. "I don't like the sound of that."

"It didn't feel great either."

"Not just that. Did you consider that the men who abused those women might come to take revenge on you?"

"Not until now." He drags his finger under the hem of my shirt, touching my bare skin. "My main focus was getting *you* in a class, and helping other women who had been hurt as well."

"Thank you," I whisper. "Being there every week has done wonders for me."

"And for others, too. I should have considered the possibility that I'd be pissing off some husbands and boyfriends."

"I guess it's just a part of the territory."

He nods thoughtfully.

"Ethan suggested that we put in some security cameras outside, and I don't think it's a bad idea."

"Did you get some shots in on them too?"

"No, there were four of them."

"What?" I sit up straight, staring at him in surprise. "Jesus, Ben, they could have killed you."

"Now you're just insulting me." He cocks an eyebrow and I can't help but chuckle.

"This isn't funny. Don't make me laugh."

"I know, it isn't funny."

I lean back into him, and he winces. I lift the side of his shirt and suck in a breath at the sight of a big black bruise there. My eyes find his.

"Looks like one of them got in a good shot to my ribs."

"I think you should soak in some Epsom salts," I inform him. "I have some."

"Only if you soak with me."

"No distracting me with sex, mister. You're hurt."

"Trust me when I say, I'm never too hurt to want to be inside of you, Savannah."

I blink rapidly, not sure how to reply to that, so I

just stand and walk quickly up to my master bathroom. I turn on the hot water in the tub, dump in about a cup of the Epsom salts and turn to find Ben leaning against the doorjamb, his muscular arms crossed over his chest, watching me intently.

"See something you like?"

He nods twice.

"The bath?"

He shakes his head no.

"The Epsom salts?"

No again. Finally, he walks to me and turns me to face the mirror. He stands behind me and leans in to kiss my neck, sending a chain reaction of shivers through me.

"I loved the way you just leaned over the tub," he whispers.

"Yep, you're a man."

His gaze finds mine in the mirror as he starts stripping me out of my clothes.

"*You're* the one who's supposed to be getting naked," I inform him, but don't try to stop him when he pulls my shirt over my head.

"It's way more fun when we're both naked, Angel."

"I can't argue with that."

After quickly stripping out of his clothes, we both get into the bath, leaning against opposite corners and watching the other. He sinks down and closes his eyes, and I follow suit.

"This feels so good," I whisper. "I don't take enough baths."

"I'll run you one every night if you like," he murmurs. I open my eyes to find him watching me lazily, but the intense look in his gaze makes my pussy pulse in attention.

"That sounds nice."

His lips twitch and he reaches for my foot, digs his thumb into my arch, and makes me moan in pleasure.

"Speaking of nice things."

"Moan like that again and I'll fuck you here in the tub."

My eyes snap open at his gruff, sexy tone. He's watching his own hands rub up and down my calf, then back to my foot. His hands are just...*magic.* Pure sexy magic.

"So I called your tattoo guy." I'm leaning back against the tub, my eyes closed, enjoying the hot water and Ben's amazing fingers on my body.

"Oh?"

"Yeah." *Dear fucking hell, don't stop rubbing my calf like that.* "I rescheduled my appointment for tomorrow afternoon."

He doesn't say anything in response, so I open one eye so I can see him. There's a crease between his eyebrows from concentrating on his task at hand.

"Did you hear me?"

"I did."

"Will you go with me? Please?"

His eyes roam up my body, skimming over every curve, until they find mine.

"I thought you said that you didn't want me to see you get it?"

"I did say that." I sink down farther into the hot water. "But I changed my mind. I'm allowed to do that."

"Yes, ma'am. What time?"

"Two."

He switches to my other foot, and part of me feels a little guilty. He's the one who got beat up tonight, and I'm the one getting pampered.

"I can take you," he says. "Would you like to go visit my mom with me before? I'd like to look in on her and see how Sally's doing with her."

"I would love that."

"Deal."

We're quiet for a long while. Just the sound of the water fills the room as Ben continues to massage my foot and leg, until finally, I just can't stand it anymore.

I need him.

*Right now.*

He's surprised when I pull my foot away, and then his eyes heat up when I move over to him, not giving even one fuck that some water splashes over the rim of the tub, and straddle him. My hands roam up his arms and shoulders and I settle myself down, pressing against the length of his already hard cock.

"I hate that you were hurt tonight," I whisper against his lips. "I'm trying to take care of you, but instead you're sharing your bath with me and rubbing *my* feet."

"No one's keeping score, Angel."

I lift my hips up and then slowly sink down onto him, taking him fully inside me, and then sit still while he kisses me senseless. He wraps his arms around me, hugging me to him, and then those amazing hands of his take a trip up my back, down my sides, and to my ass. He grips me, not gently, and guides me in a slow up and down rhythm, keeping us both teetering on the edge of sanity.

He's staring into my eyes, breathing hard, as I ride him. Finally, I can't stand it anymore. I push down and grind my clit on his pubic bone, leaning my forehead against his as the orgasm shudders through me. I'm still quivering when he stiffens and succumbs himself.

I push my fingers through his hair and kiss his cheeks, his nose, his forehead.

"You are the best part of my life," he whispers.

"Same." I smile. "Same."

# CHAPTER 12

~BEN~

"So that's your outfit today?" I ask as she pushes her sunglasses onto her face and reaches for her purse.

"Yeah." She looks down at herself and then up at me with a frown. "What's wrong with it?"

"There's nothing wrong with it, but I'm going to be thinking about getting you *out* of it all fucking day and we're going to see my mom."

She smirks and saunters out of her house ahead of me, her chin up and stride confident. She's in some sexy blue heels with black pants and a hot black and white flowy shirt thing that gives me hints of her curves as she moves.

I already know what's under the shirt, and I want my hands on it.

I never stop wanting her, no matter what she's wearing.

"I'm quite sure you can keep your hands to yourself while we visit your mama," she says as we pull away from her house. "You're a strong man."

"Strong enough to rip that shirt off of you so I can get my mouth on you," I murmur and enjoy the look of pure lust and surprise she tosses me from the passenger seat. "It's no secret that I want you."

"No, I just have to get used to you *saying* it."

"I plan to say it a lot, and I'm not going to censor myself when we're alone. I don't want you to either."

"Trust me, I don't censor myself. And being surprised now and again is fun. But now I'm sitting here with wet panties and we're about to go see your mom."

Now it's my turn to toss her a surprised glance. Fucking hell she's sexy, and when words like those leave her plump red lips, all I can think of doing is pulling this car over and fucking her right here in the driver's seat of my car.

"We'll make up for it later," I promise as I pull into my mom's driveway. Before she can get out of the car, I pull her to me and kiss the fuck out of her. I'm rock hard, and even though I just had her this morning, I want her again. "This evening, I'm going to do things to you that you didn't even know were possible."

"Do I need a safe word?" she asks, her lips tipped in a smirk.

"Never. You're always safe with me."

She rolls her eyes and reaches for the door handle.

"Obviously. But maybe you want to try some butt stuff, and in that case, I'll have to say *purple.*"

"Why purple?"

"Because I hate the color purple almost as much as I hate butt stuff."

I frown, immediately wondering if that was her safe word with the asshole, or how much anal play he made her engage in, and it makes my head feel like it's going to explode.

"Don't overthink it," she says and cups my cheek in her hand. "I'm playing with you."

"I know. But we should probably have a conversation soon."

She nods. "Probably. But first, we're going to visit your mama, and then I'm getting some new ink."

She smiles like a young girl excited for Christmas morning and then pulls herself out of my car.

I take a deep, cleansing breath and follow behind her.

Sally opens the door with a warm smile. "Hey, Ben."

"Hi, Sally. This is Savannah."

Sally shakes Van's hand and steps back so we can walk inside. "Your mama is in the living room."

I nod and find Mom sitting at a card table, putting a puzzle together. Her injured foot is up on a stool.

"Hi, sweet boy," she says with a happy smile. I lean down and kiss her cheek. "Oh, you brought my favorite Boudreaux with you."

"We're all your favorites," Van says and gives Mom a hug. "How are you feeling?"

"Oh, just fine." Mom waves her question off and points to the chairs facing her. "Have a seat, you two."

"Just let me know if you need anything," Sally says before discreetly leaving the three of us to talk.

Van and I sit next to each other and I immediately reach for her hand, threading our fingers together. I kiss her knuckles and glance up to see my mom smiling widely, watching us closely.

"Well, isn't that lovely."

"I told you on the phone that Van and I were seeing each other."

"Yes, but now I can see it with my own two eyes." She shifts in her chair. "And let me just say, it's about damn time."

"Not you too," Savannah says with a short laugh. "You sound just like my family."

"None of us are blind, child," she says gently. "Your mama and I have talked about the two of you for years."

"So everyone talks about us behind our backs," Van says with sass, making Mom laugh.

"Of course we do, darlin'. We're southern women."

"I've missed you, Miss Millie. I need to come see you more often."

"Well, that would be a delight." She shifts her gaze to me. "What happened to your face?"

"I have a split lip."

"I can see that. How did you get it?"

"Some guy threw a punch," I reply, evading the question as much as possible. Mama worries enough already. "I ended it."

"In class?"

"Yes," I lie. Van tightens her grip on my hand, but I don't elaborate on the story and Mom is already asking questions about the other siblings and how the businesses are going.

"Has Gabby been busy out at the inn?" she asks and smiles at Sally when she comes in with a tray of tea and cookies. "Thank you, dear."

"My pleasure." Sally leaves the room again, and I swoop in for a couple of cookies.

"These are damn good."

"Sally is an excellent cook," Mom says and takes a bite of a cookie. "But back to the inn."

"I think they're pretty busy," Van says and pours herself some tea. "This is a slower season, so she might have a night or two here and there that she's not full, but I know that the business is thriving."

"That's wonderful," Mom replies. "I'm so happy that she's turned that big house into something special. It was always a beautiful home, but now that all of you are grown up, and your daddy's gone, your mama wouldn't have much use for it."

"I'm happy that it's stayed in the family," Van agrees. "And Gabby has really made it beautiful. You and my mom should make a reservation and go spend a weekend out there."

"Oh, that would be wonderful. I'll mention it to her."

"I would like to hear how you're doing with Sally," Van says and takes a sip of her tea. "She seems nice."

"She really is a nice woman," Mom says.

"Of course, you wouldn't say anything bad about a person even if they *weren't* nice," Van says. "I know how you are, Miss Millie."

"Well, there's no need to talk ill of people," Mom reminds us both. "But I can honestly say that Sally is a delight to have around. She's smart, and she cooks very well. She doesn't let me win at cards, and she likes some of the same shows as me."

"That's great," Van says. She leans over to squeeze my mom's hand.

My God, I love this woman. She adores my mom, and genuinely worries for her. She's completely focused on being in the moment with Mom right now, and I'm surprised to realize that I don't think I've ever been more attracted to her as I am in this moment.

She's not just beautiful and everything I could ever want in bed.

She's thoughtful and kind.

And she's *mine.*

"I told Ben I wanted to come here as soon as possible to make sure that Sally is treating you well."

"Oh yes, we're just fine. I wasn't sure about having someone here all the time. I don't need a babysitter, and your mama is just next door. But I admit that it's nice to have the company. And she leaves just after dinner, so that gives me a couple of hours to myself before bed."

"That's perfect," Van says with a relieved smile. "And how is your foot healing up?"

"You know me, I'm always slow to heal, but it's not giving me too much trouble. I just walk slow, and with a cane. And let me tell you something, that cane has got to go as soon as possible. I look like an old woman with it."

"You're beautiful," I murmur. Mom's cheeks pinken and she winks at me.

"You're a charmer. Is that how he snagged you, Savannah?"

"Actually, no. He wasn't terribly charming when we decided to give this a go."

"Really?" Mom frowns at me. "I taught him better than that."

"Actually," Savannah continues, "he was great. He wasn't charming, but he was honest, and he's always nothing but considerate and gentle with me."

"That's better," Mom says with a satisfied nod. "Good boy."

I laugh as Van's phone rings. "I'm so glad that my mom doesn't treat me like I'm fourteen."

The sarcasm is thick in my voice.

"I'm sorry, I have to take this call. It's the office." Van stands and walks out of the room, already focused on whomever has called.

"You're not a child. You're a man, and you're treating this lovely girl the way a man should treat her. I'm proud of you for that."

"Are we going to talk about our feelings all day?"

Mom rolls her eyes and then just smiles at me. "Now that she's occupied, how is it really going?"

"She's amazing," I reply honestly. My mom has always been easy to talk to. "I knew years ago that she was special. We all knew it."

"We did," she confirms, and quietly waits for me to continue.

"But she's more." I rub my hand through my hair, trying to think of words that adequately describe how I feel for Savannah. "She's everything."

Mom smiles. "I certainly hope you plan to marry her. I want grandchildren."

I laugh and nod. "It's still early, but yes. I plan to be with her for the rest of my life. I don't know about kids, but she's it for me."

"I'm so happy for you both," Mom says just as Savannah returns.

"I'm sorry about that," she says and tosses her phone in her bag, then sits in her chair. "Did I miss anything good?"

"He's just telling me secrets," Mom says and then laughs when Van stares at me with wide eyes. "I'm kidding. I'm so happy you both stopped in today. I'd like to see you more often."

"I'd like that too," Savannah says with a nod. "You should come to Mama's house for dinner this Sunday."

"I think I might just do that," Mom replies and smiles again when she sees Van reach out for my hand. She's probably already planned the whole damn wedding in her head.

Savannah checks the time.

"I hate to cut this short, but my appointment is in about a half hour."

"We should go," I reply. "Just call me if you need anything. I've already given Sally the same order, and she has my cell number."

"I'm fine." Mom tilts her head, waiting for me to kiss her cheek. "Go live your life, my boy."

"SALLY SEEMS REALLY GREAT," Van says as we pull out of Mom's driveway and head to her appointment at my ink shop. "And professional, which is key."

"I agree. I'm comfortable with her being there. Much more comfortable than when Mom was by herself."

Van nods.

"I have a confession."

I glance over at her and then back to the road. "Okay."

"I don't like needles."

I frown. "You've had a tattoo before."

185

"I know, and I didn't like it then either, but it was on the back of my neck, so I couldn't see it."

"Where are you getting this one?"

She shakes her head and keeps talking, evading my question.

"So, I might be freaking out a bit. I'm not ridiculous. I don't pass out or throw up or anything."

"That's encouraging."

"But I *really* don't like them."

"And you were going to do this by yourself?"

She scowls. "Well, yeah. I'm not a weanie, Ben."

I'm unable to hold the burst of laughter in. "No. That you're not."

"Stop trying to distract me."

"You're going to be fine, Van. I'll be there to hold your hand."

She smiles. "That's nice of you."

"Yeah, I'm a nice guy."

She snorts and shakes her head. "And humble."

"That, too."

I pull into the parking lot and follow Van inside. My guy, Buck, is standing at the counter.

"Hey, man," Buck says and shakes my hand. "I can't take you as a walk in today. I have an appointment right now."

"I'm your appointment," Van says. "And he's with me."

Buck cocks a brow. "Savannah?"

"Yep."

"Nice to meet you." He holds his hand out for hers and she immediately shakes it. "Do you have what you want with you?"

"I do." She reaches in her handbag and takes out a folded piece of paper. She smoothes it out and passes it to Buck. "I want exactly this."

"This won't take long at all. Where do you want it?"

She glances at me, and then says, "On my side, like this." She gestures on her side, up and down, and I cringe.

That's gonna hurt.

"We can do that," Spider says with a nod. "I'm gonna go in the back and make a stencil for this and we'll get started."

"Great."

Savannah links her fingers with mine and holds on tight. She's nervous, but aside from the vise grip on my hand, you'd never know it.

She looks cool and calm.

I lean down and whisper in her ear. "You're doing great."

"Nothing's happened yet," she reminds me.

In just a few minutes, Buck returns with a wet sten-cil. He gestures for Van to lie on his table, on her side, and she pulls her shirt up under her armpit.

She's not wearing a bra.

Fuck me.

"I'm going to put this on you, and then you can go

187

look in the mirror to make sure you like it. We can move it as many times as you need."

"Okay," Van says with a smile. Buck presses the stencil on, and when he removes the paper, I can see what it says.

*Still I rise.*

The font is simple. It's not swirly or overtly feminine.

It's perfect for her.

She stands and looks in the mirror, and comes back with a big smile on that gorgeous face of hers.

"This is great. Exactly what I had in mind."

"Okay, let's get to work then."

She lies back down and I sit so she's facing me. Buck is sitting behind her. I take her hand and kiss her knuckles.

"Ready?" I ask.

"Yes." She bites her lip when Buck starts the tattoo machine.

"It's just noise."

She nods and grips my hand tighter as Buck begins. I kiss her forehead and then her cheek and I can't resist whispering in her ear.

"You're so fucking sexy." The words are barely audible, but she bites her lip again at my words, and I know she can hear me.

I don't want Buck to hear me.

"You amaze me every day. This tattoo is beautiful."

"It's important," she whispers back, and I feel my

heart catch. This tattoo is a reminder to herself of what she's been through, and she rose above it.

"So important," I agree.

"Jesus, they weren't lying when they said rib tattoos hurt." She holds her breath. "My neck wasn't nearly this bad."

"We're half done already," Buck replies. "And you're doing great."

"See? I told you." I kiss her lips softly. "Breathe, Angel."

She takes a deep breath and lets it out slowly. "Keep talking. It distracts me."

I lower my lips to her ear again and keep whispering. Jesus, I had no idea that watching her get ink could turn me on like this. I feel like this is just as intimate as anything else we've shared.

"I want you," I whisper. "I want you every day. And I'm not talking about sex, sweetheart. I want *you*."

She smiles softly.

"I want you, too."

"You have the cutest little freckle under your arm," I continue. "I want to kiss you there."

"The freckle would like that."

"There are a thousand other things I want to do to you."

"We have plenty of time for you to do those things," she says around a wince when Buck glides the needle over a particularly tender spot. "Is he almost done?"

"I'm done," Buck says and soaks a piece of gauze

and washes the excess ink off. "You can go look in the mirror before I cover it."

She jumps up and hurries to the mirror, then grins happily at Buck's handiwork.

"It's perfect. I *love* it."

"Good." Buck covers the wound and gives her instructions on after care. "You have this guy for questions. He's an expert at tattoo care."

"I've done my research," she says and passes him her credit card. "Thank you so much."

"My pleasure."

"Are you sore?" I ask as we settle into my car and drive away.

"A little," she says. "But it's not bad. It's not a huge tattoo."

"It'll heal fast. What are your plans for the weekend?"

"Household chores, mostly. Laundry and grocery shopping. I thought I might read a bit."

"Spend it with me."

She smiles. "I was hoping you'd say that."

"I'm taking the weekend off of the gym," I reply. "I need to stop by there to wrap up a couple of things for the week and then I'm all yours."

"While you do that, why don't I run home and gather some things for the weekend? It'll be easier than bouncing back and forth for clothes and stuff."

"I love a woman who knows how to multi-task."

"Women are experts at multi-tasking," she reminds me. "But I'll need to borrow your Jeep."

"No problem." I pull up in front of my building and leave the keys in it as we both get out and meet on the sidewalk for a long kiss. "Drive safely."

"Yes, sir."

Her lips twitch in humor.

"I'll be done here in about thirty minutes."

"That's perfect timing." She kisses me once more and then walks around the car to the driver's side, tossing me a sassy smile as she opens the door. "I'll see you in a little bit."

I wave as she pulls away and then walk inside where it's cool. There is one class in session, and another private lesson going on in the smaller dojo. Ethan is at the desk scowling at the computer.

"This credit card system is fucking annoying," he says.

"Hello to you too," I reply. "Get Bethany to do that stuff. That's what I pay her for." Bethany is our office girl, and she's been with us for over a year. She's good at her job.

"I gave her the night off. She and her husband have a wedding to go to tonight."

"What about—" My phone rings, and I glance at the screen. It's Van. "Hi, sweetheart."

"Ben?" She's crying, and I'm instantly on high alert.

"What's wrong?"

"I... I..."

"Slow down. What happened?"

"I'm so sorry, Ben."

"Where are you?"

"About a mile from my house."

"I'm coming to find you. Don't hang up, Angel. Do you hear me?"

"Yes."

Ethan throws me his car keys and I run out to his car. My heart is beating so fast that I can barely hear her through the rushing in my ears.

"Did you get into an accident?"

"I guess so."

"Van? Talk to me, baby."

"The brakes wouldn't work," she says and my blood runs cold. "I had to stop, but they wouldn't work."

I can see my Jeep up ahead, plowed into a traffic signal pole.

"I'm here. I'm right here."

# CHAPTER 13

~SAVANNAH~

*B*en waves me off in the rear view mirror as I pull away from the curb, headed to my house. How long can we continue to maintain two houses? I mean, I don't want to jump the gun or anything, and I know it seems fast, but I don't want to sleep without him. We spend almost every night together anyway.

But the thought of selling my beautiful house, especially now that it's finished being remodeled, doesn't excite me. And I know that Ben has put a lot of work into his house too. It's perfect for him. I doubt he would want to sell it.

And if this is the biggest *issue* in our relationship, I'd say we're doing very well.

I smirk as the light ahead turns yellow and then red. I press my foot on the brake, but nothing happens.

*Nothing fucking happens.*

I grip the wheel tightly and try again, but his car won't stop. It's not even slowing down, certainly not enough to stop at the light.

"Oh my God."

I can't go through the intersection; I'll cause a huge accident. There's no one on the sidewalk, thank God, so I jerk the wheel and aim for a signal post, hitting it squarely.

The airbag deploys, smacking me in the face. I see stars and shake my head. Jesus, that hurt.

But all I can do is worry that I could have hurt someone.

"Are you okay?" Someone yells through the window. I try to open the door, but my fingers are shaking so violently, I can't grip the door handle. Is that me breathing like I just ran a marathon?

"Open it!" I yell, and the stranger complies. The door opens, letting in fresh air and the smell of a crushed front end. "Damn it."

"Hey, are you okay?" The stranger asks again, his voice full of concern. He lays his hand on my shoulder, not hard but with authority, making me stay in my seat when I would jump out of the car to survey the damage. "Is anything broken?"

"I don't think so," I immediately reply and feel tears spring to my eyes. "Oh my God."

"It's okay," the stranger says. "I'll stay with you until you calm down and someone comes to get you."

"You're nice," I whisper and struggle to calm my

breathing. "Why didn't the brakes work?"

"Excellent question," he says grimly and I reach for my phone to call Ben.

"Hi, sweetheart."

"Ben?" Just the sound of his voice triggers the tears. I'm suddenly sobbing, and I can't control it. I can barely speak, and I can't pull any air into my lungs.

"What's wrong?" His voice is on edge now, worried.

"I... I..."

"Slow down. What happened?"

"I'm so sorry, Ben."

"Where are you?"

"About a mile from my house."

"I'm coming to find you. Don't hang up, Angel. Do you hear me?"

*Thank God.* Yes, come find me!

"Yes."

"Did you get into an accident?"

"I guess so." I glance around, but the airbag is in my way. I can barely see cars drive past and people gawking through their windows. Someone takes a picture. There are voices, but the stranger stands quietly next to me.

"Van? Talk to me, baby."

"The brakes wouldn't work," I say as I try to catch my breath and calm down. "I had to stop, but they wouldn't work."

"I'm here." I spin around, looking for him, but I don't see him. I step out of the car now, and the

195

stranger must be convinced that I'm okay because he steps away, allowing me past him. "I'm right here," Ben says.

A car I don't recognize parks behind Ben's Jeep and Ben jumps out of the driver's side, running at me.

"Ben."

"I'm here," he says again and grips my shoulders in his hands, studying my face. "Are you hurt?"

"I don't think so. Just scared."

He looks me over, satisfied with what he sees. I can hear sirens coming.

"Did someone call the police?" Ben calls out.

"I did," the stranger who's been with me says, making me frown. I didn't hear him do that. "They're on the way."

"Thank you," Ben says. He's rubbing circles on my back, and I'm finally calming down. I wipe the tears from my face. "What happened?" he asks me.

"I pressed the brakes and they just didn't respond." I frown and study the steaming front end of his car. "I couldn't chance running the light and hitting another car, so—"

"You did the right thing," he says immediately and pulls me to him in the best hug ever. His hands are strong on my back, and his chest is solid against my cheek. "Are you sure you're okay?"

"I'm fine," I reply and kiss his sternum before looking up at him. "Just shook up. Airbags aren't fun. I'm sorry about your car."

"Fuck the car," he says with a shake of the head. "You're all I'm worried about, Angel."

And cue the damn butterflies. Not to mention, tears are threatening again, but I take a deep breath and truly take mental stock of my body. My shoulder is a bit sore from the seatbelt, but otherwise I really do physically feel fine.

The police arrive and for the next thirty minutes I'm caught up in the hustle and bustle of giving a statement, Ben calling for a tow truck, and then handing me the phone with Beau on the other end.

"Vanny?" Beau asks. "Are you okay?"

"Ben told you I am," I reply. The adrenaline has slowed down with the distraction of the police.

"I wanted to hear it from your mouth, sugar. Do you need anything?"

"No, we have it all under control. Thanks for asking, though."

*Ben has it all under control.* But I'm proud of the way I didn't fall apart. I mean, I had a moment because I'm a normal woman, but after the initial shock, I actually felt *fine.* Not scared shitless that Ben will hurt me because I broke his car, or yell at me, or shame me.

He's caring for me, and it's the sexiest thing he could ever do.

I end the call with Beau and once the tow truck takes the car away and the police leave, Ben leads me to the strange car and takes me to my house.

"Who's car is this?"

"Ethan's," he says, a muscle in his jaw ticking as he pulls into my driveway.

"Are you mad at me?"

"Not even a little bit," he replies before he cuts the engine and helps me out of the car and leads me up to my door. He waits while I unlock it and then follows me in. "You grab your things for this weekend and then we'll take your car back to my place."

"What about Ethan's car?"

"I'll arrange to have it returned to him." He cups my face in his hands, and for the first time in my life, I see true fear in Ben's eyes. "My God, you scared me."

"Scared me too," I whisper. "Have you had any issues with your brakes?"

"No." His voice is flat. "I'll have it fixed and sell it. I won't have you drive it again. I can't take the chance that this could happen again."

"I'm sure it's just a fluke."

"I don't give a fuck. You could have been hurt, or killed, and I won't take that chance again." He tips his forehead to rest on mine. "I'm so sorry, my love."

"I'm fine," I assure him and rub my hands up and down his back. "You took care of me."

"That's my job," he says. His eyes are closed, but his body is still tight with adrenaline. I didn't think it was possible to find him even *more* attractive than I did this morning, but fuck me, I want him.

"This might be the adrenaline talking," I say as I

walk him backward until his back hits my front door. "But I need to do something."

He opens his eyes and frowns. "Okay."

I nod and kiss him deeply, my fingernails digging into his arms as the kiss goes from hot to inferno in about three seconds. Finally, I pull away and kiss my way down his black T-shirt, to his belly. I unbutton his pants and am pleased to find that he's not wearing any underwear. That sexy as hell piece of metal is winking at me.

"Van." His voice is husky, full of lust. "You don't have to."

"Oh yeah. I do." He's already hard and heavy in my hand. The skin is smooth, and what he can do with this is ridiculous.

I'm about to thank him in the best way possible.

I lick the length of him, from balls to tip. I want to take it slow. To soak in the sounds he makes, and the way his cock twitches at my touch, but this moment isn't for slow and easy. I'm too excited. I'm too revved up.

So I sink over him as far as I can and then I wrap my lips around him and pull up, my hand following the motion. His hands are fisted in my hair, he's groaning words that I can't make out, and I fucking love it.

I feel sexy and powerful as this strong, alpha man becomes putty in my hands.

And mouth.

"I'm going to come, Angel."

I nod without skipping a beat, but he curses.

"Seriously, Van, I'm going to lose it and I don't want to do it in your mouth."

"Do it," I reply and go back to licking and sucking, urging him on. He sucks air in through his teeth.

"Jesus Christ Almighty, you're good at this."

I smile brilliantly on the inside, not skipping a beat, and he suddenly comes, quivering with his release.

"My God, Van."

"No, I'm no god," I reply with a sassy smile as I stand and he zips up his pants. He's watching me intently, his eyes on fire. "I just couldn't help myself. You're sexy as fuck, Ben."

"I want you," he says. His voice is deceptively calm and low. He stalks toward me, and I walk backwards. Not trying to get away from him, but wanting to see where he's going with this. When my back hits a wall, he cages me in, leaning his hands on the wall at the side of my head. He kisses my forehead.

"Look at me."

I comply, looking up at his handsome face. I can't help but cup his face in my hands and enjoy the way the stubble feels against my palms.

"Hi," I say. He smiles slowly, and then chuckles just before he kisses me soundly.

"You're just full of surprises, Angel."

"Well, I don't want to be boring."

He shakes his head, his eyes pinned to my lips.

"You're never boring. And I don't know what I did to deserve that, but I'll do my best to do it more often."

It's my turn to laugh. "Let's say it was a combination of adrenaline and lust."

"So we have to become avid thrill seekers."

"No," I reply. "I don't need thrills to want you."

"I want you every minute of every day," he says. "I'd love nothing more than to boost you up against this wall and have my way with you."

"Seems like a waste to not take advantage of this wall. It's just standing here. We should use it for something."

"You're quite the smart ass today. I like it."

I just smile and feel the loss when he pulls away from me.

"Come. Let's get your things and get out of here. I want to take you out tonight, if you're feeling up to it. If you're not, we can just watch a movie or something."

"Like, on a real date?"

"Yes, ma'am."

"Cool!" I do a little shimmy before I head up to my bedroom to pack. I'm definitely up for it. I feel like I could be up for anything right now. Adrenaline really is a thing. "Thanks for the heads up. I'll pack a pretty dress."

"Don't forget the heels!" he calls after me.

"Have you met me?" I yell back and smile at the sound of his laugh.

Tonight is going to be *fun.*

~

IT'S WINDY THIS EVENING. I wore a flowy organza dress that I love because of the pretty yellow flowers embroidered in the material. But it doesn't match well with wind.

I might flash someone, or everyone, in the Quarter, and that would be bad. Much to my ex-husband's disappointment, I'm not an exhibitionist.

But here in the restaurant, I'm comfortable and feel sexy in this dress with my red peep-toe stilettos and my hair twisted up off of my neck. Ben keeps brushing his fingertips over the skin at the base of my neck, sending shivers down my whole body and puckering my nipples.

We're waiting at the bar for our table to be ready, sipping a drink and just enjoying being close to each other.

"You're sure you're up to this?" he asks.

"Ben, I'm fine. My shoulders are a little sore from tensing up and the seatbelt, but other than that, I feel good. Also, you've asked me that about seven times. If I didn't want to be here, I'd tell you."

"Okay," he says and kisses my temple. "You look so beautiful."

I grin as he presses his lips to my ear. "I'll be right back."

He might as well have just said, *take all of your clothes off.*

"Okay." I smile at him as he saunters away and take a sip of my lemon drop. Kate got me hooked on these when she moved to New Orleans a couple of years ago. I don't drink often, but I think I've earned one or two of these after the day I just had.

"Hey there, sweet thing."

I glance to my left to find a middle-aged, balding man standing next to me. He has something black stuck between his two front teeth.

I don't reply, but he keeps talking.

"How many drinks do you think it would take to get you to come home with me?"

*Lord Jesus.*

I roll my eyes and turn to face him. He's grinning, showing off that hideous hunk of food in his teeth. "There isn't enough liquor in this bar to make that happen."

His smile slips. "So I should just keep on walking by then?"

"Oh yeah. For sure."

I turn away just in time to see Ben sit next to me. My shoulders relax in relief. Not because I couldn't handle that jerk by myself. Because I could have. And I did.

"Who was that?" Ben asks.

"Absolutely nobody," I reply just as the hostess comes to tell us our table is ready. It's tucked in the corner of the dimly lit restaurant. There's a candle burning on the table for two and it feels intimate and romantic as we sit and look over the menu. The waitress refills our drinks and takes our order and Ben takes my hand, kissing the knuckles.

"You look nice." I sigh in pleasure and look him up and down. He's in a black button down with the sleeves rolled, showing off his tattoos, and a pair of black pants that hug his ass in the most delicious way.

"You are stunning," he replies. "You didn't disappoint with those shoes."

"These are some of my favorites," I agree and stick my foot out from under the table so I can admire them. "It also helps that you're so tall and I'm so short so I can wear any height of heel that I want."

"That must be a woman problem."

"Absolutely." I nod and sip my drink. "I know that some women don't care if they're taller than their guy, but I prefer a tall man. Not that it's ever been much of an issue for me. All of us Boudreaux girls are petite."

"Your mama is tiny," he reminds me and I nod again.

"This is nice."

"I should take you out more often."

"I'm not complaining," I reply. "By the time we're both out of work at the end of the day, we're tired. I like just being with you in the evenings."

"I do too. But some of this is nice now and again as well."

"I won't argue," I say as our food is delivered. "Have you heard from the garage about your car yet?"

"I'm not expecting to hear from them until Monday. I hope you don't mind if we use your car for the next few days."

"I don't mind at all."

We enjoy our dinner, and each other, chatting while we inhale our meal. I didn't realize how hungry I was until the food arrived.

"Can I interest you in any dessert?" The waitress asks.

"No, thanks." I shake my head and sip the last of my drink. "I'm stuffed."

"Just the check, please," Ben says, smiling at me. "How do you feel?"

"A little buzzed," I admit. "How many of these did I have?"

"Three."

"Yep, that'll do it." I giggle and then cover my mouth with my napkin. "I promise not to embarrass you with my drunken antics."

"You're not drunk, and you would never embarrass me."

I snort and gather my clutch as we leave the restaurant. Ben's right, I'm not drunk, but I do feel mighty fuzzy and I can't say that I don't like it.

"You've seen me drunk more than you should," I inform him. I have to hold my dress down as we walk to my car so the wind doesn't whip it up over my head and I give a few people a show. "But I'm not an alcoholic. I promise."

"You're fun when you're buzzed," he says with a laugh. "And I've loved that you would call me when you needed a ride home. Who cares if you drink a little with the girls, or with me, now and again? The important thing is that you're safe."

"You say pretty things with that pretty mouth of yours," I reply as the wind kicks up again, sending my skirt almost up to my waist. "This must be what Marilyn Monroe felt like over that grate." I hurry into the passenger side of my car and sigh in relief when Ben closes the door and hurries around to the other side. "I didn't want to show everyone the goods."

"The goods?" He asks with a raised brow.

"You know, the *goods*. You've been quite intimate with the goods as of late. The parts that only you are supposed to see."

"Ah, yes, the goods." He grins and leans over to kiss me. "You make me laugh, Savannah."

"Ditto." I kiss his nose. "Are you going to ask me to show other people the goods?"

His eyes narrow for a moment and then he just slowly shakes his head from side to side. "No, ma'am."

"Good." I settle back against the seat as he starts the car and pulls away from the curb. "The jackass used to do that." I cringe. "I'm sorry. I'm sure you don't want to hear that."

"Actually, I'd like to hear anything you'd like to tell me."

"Most of it is embarrassing."

"Let's get something straight right now, Angel. There is never a reason for you to be embarrassed with me. I love you, heart and soul, and nothing is ever going to change that. I want to know about your past, even if it's hard to listen to because it helps me understand you better."

"You're wonderful," I whisper. It's a good thing I had all those drinks. I'd never have the balls to talk about this with him otherwise. Not the way I need to. And not because I think Ben would judge me, or be repulsed by me. No, it's because even I can't believe I put up with it for all of that time.

But it's dark, and the car is quiet, and Ben makes me feel safe.

"He was just mean," I begin. "I mean, that's the root of it all. He wasn't always. Certainly not at first because if that had been the case I never would have stayed with him. Thanks to a lot of counseling, I've learned that he just likes to humiliate. He's good at it. He threatens, but his threats aren't idle. He will follow through."

"What kind of threats?" Ben asks softly as he pulls into his driveway. Neither of us makes a move to get out of the car and I'm relieved.

"Oh, you know." I shrug. "He would say that if I didn't wear what he told me to he'd find a way to humiliate me in public. Or if I didn't work harder at making my stomach flat he'd kick my ass."

"Kick your ass?"

"Oh yeah. Literally. He was careful not to leave bruises where everyone could see them. I guess that's normal."

"No," he says. I can't see his face in the darkness, but his voice is hard. "It's not normal at all, baby."

"For men like that I mean. Kate once told me that her first husband was the same way. But anyway, he was into some things, some fetishes, that I wasn't into. He would get *so mad* at me. He didn't like to be told no.

"At first he'd just act all disappointed, and make me feel about two inches tall. Guilt trip city." I roll my eyes, no longer upset or afraid of what he did to me, and now just disgusted. "As time passed, he'd just make me do it anyway."

"Fucking hell," Ben says. He's gripping the steering wheel with both hands. If there was light in here, I'd see that his knuckles are white.

"I can stop."

"No, let's finish it."

I nod and swallow hard. The liquor is wearing off.

"One of his favorite things was exhibitionism. I do *not* like even the idea of strangers, or anyone, watching me have sex or be naked. It doesn't interest me at all. And I know that some people do like it, and that's totally fine. But I don't. I'm not going to give you all of the details because you don't need it in your head, but let's just say that I did things I didn't want to. Mostly because I was avoiding the punishment that came with saying no. But then I got both anyway, so it was all just a shit show."

"I should have killed him."

"That's not the first time you've said that."

I slip out of my seatbelt and climb over the console so I can straddle Ben's lap and look him in the eyes.

"I'm not telling you this to piss you off or so you want to hurt him again. I'm *not*. Do you have any idea what the past few weeks have meant to me, Ben? Before we started this, I was unsure of myself and I was afraid that I'd never be able to be intimate with someone ever again. Because to do that, you have to *trust* and he ruined that part of me.

"Until you. You've made me feel powerful and beautiful. I know that you respect me and my boundaries, and that you only have me and my best interests in mind. What I had before was dark and evil and *wrong*. It wasn't love. It was *never* love.

"This, right here, is love." I lean my forehead against his and sigh in happiness as his arms come around my back in a tight hug. "This is love and trust and everything good. What happened before doesn't matter, Ben. It's over, and it doesn't matter because now I have you."

"We have each other," he says, still holding me close. "And I'm never going to let anything like that happen to you again. I just have one last question, and then we're going to leave it all in the past."

"Anything."

"Why did you stay, Van? After he showed you who he really was, why did you stay?"

I can feel the tears want to come, but I'll be damned if I give Lance even one more ounce of control.

"Because he threatened my family."

"He fucking blackmailed you into marrying him?"

I nod once and then shake my head in horror. "I just love you all so much—"

"Wait. He threatened to hurt me too?"

"All of you."

Ben takes a long, deep breath and then lets it out slowly. "I don't want to make love to you tonight."

I blink rapidly and stare down at Ben in confusion.

"I want to hold you. I want to *be* with you. And I want to remind you what it feels like to be loved for *you*. For being the wonderful woman you are, and I want to show you what unconditional means."

"Oh, Ben." Now I let the tears come because they're tears of joy. "You do that every day."

"Come on." We untangle ourselves and get out of the car and walk up to the door, but when Ben takes his keys out to unlock the door, we find that it's already ajar. "I thought you said you locked this behind us when we left."

"I did," I reply. "I know I did."

"Well, it's unlocked now." His face is grim as he looks down at me. "I'm going to go in to make sure it's safe. You stay here."

"Like hell I'll stay here."

"Savannah."

"Ben." I narrow my eyes. "I'm not staying out here by myself. That's how horror movies start, and I will *not* have it."

"Right." He sighs and pulls out his phone. "Eli? Yeah. I need you at my house now." He listens and then nods. "Thanks."

"Why did you call Eli and not the cops?"

"Because I don't know that this is a break in. And if you won't stay out here by yourself, Eli will wait with you."

"I can go in. I'm perfectly capable of kicking ass."

"No." He backs me up against a pillar on the porch. "You are *everything*, Van. I'm not taking you anywhere that could be dangerous. Now damn it, you're going to wait out here with Eli while I figure out what the fuck is going on."

I can only watch his face, his hair a riot in the wind. "Okay."

"Thank you."

"For what?"

"For curbing your stubborn side."

We're both quiet as we wait, listening for any sound from inside, but everything is still.

"You're sure you locked the door?"

"I swear—"

Suddenly, there's an explosion at the side of the house; sparks fly everywhere.

"Mother fucker."

211

## CHAPTER 14

~SAVANNAH~

*E*li pulls in the driveway just after the explosion that just about gave me a heart attack.

"What in the hell is up with today?" I demand, as Eli comes running up to join us.

"What was that?" Eli asks with a scowl. "Van, go get in my car."

"Fuck that," I reply and run after them as they hurry around the side of the house. "I'm not a damsel in distress."

"Jesus, she's stubborn," Eli says. "Looks like the wind blew your transformer."

"It's been a shit day," Ben answers and rubs his hands over his face. "I need to go check out the inside of the house. The door was open when we got back from dinner."

Eli scowls. "It's not like you to leave your house unlocked."

"I pulled the door closed behind us when we left," I add. "And I know, without a doubt, that I locked it. It's habit."

"I'm not saying you didn't," Ben replies and kisses my forehead. "Which is why I don't want you going in there until I've had a look first."

"Good idea," Eli says.

"Fine," I reply, resigned. "I'll stay out here like a weak person who hasn't been training to kick ass for the past two years."

"You're the only person I know who would complain because I'm trying to keep you out of harm's way." Ben shoves his fingers through his hair as we walk to the front of the house. "Just give me ten minutes."

"We're good," Eli says with a nod. "And I'll call 911 if I see or hear anything suspicious."

Ben nods and goes into the house, turning on the flashlight on his phone, since there's no power thanks to the transformer blowing out.

"I don't like being treated like I'm weak," I mumble to Eli who just busts up laughing.

"Do you think that's what he's doing?"

"Well, yeah. I can kick ass too."

"Of course you can. But he loves you, Van. I wouldn't let Kate go in there either. Call us old fashioned, but it's our job to keep our women safe, and by God, that's what he's doing."

"Why do you have to make sense?" I demand, my irritation disappearing.

"Because I'm your big brother. I know everything."

"Whoa, that escalated quickly," I reply, making him laugh.

"It's all clear," Ben says as he walks outside. "It must have been the wind. I know you locked it and closed it, but maybe it didn't latch right and the wind blew it open."

"Could be," Eli says. "Your porch is deep enough, and there are trees out front, so it's doubtful that anyone from the street would have seen it. Especially in the dark."

Ben nods and wraps his arm around my shoulders.

"I guess we're spending the weekend at my house," I say with a grin.

"I guess so," Ben replies. "I'll run in and grab your bag."

"Leave it," I say, waving him off. "I'll need those things here anyway."

"Wait. Are you *moving in together*?" Eli asks.

Ben laughs and I just shrug. "No one said that. But we're together most nights, Eli."

"Yeah, okay," Eli says, not at all impressed. "I'm going home."

We wave him off and climb into my car.

"I'll call the electrician and power company in the morning," Ben says. "It's been a hell of a day."

"It has," I agree and take his hand in mine, linking our fingers. "Let's just hibernate at my place this weekend. We can order pizza and Chinese and watch movies. Make love. Just chill."

"Best weekend plans I've ever heard." He kisses my hand. "I think it's important for you to be naked during most of it."

"If I have to be naked, so do you."

"Of course. I wouldn't expect you to be naked alone. There's no fun in that."

"BEST WEEKEND EVER," I say to Charly. I'm on the phone with her Monday afternoon as I get ready to go to class. "We didn't even leave my house."

"I love those weekends," Charly says. "I'm happy that things are going well."

"Is it possible that they could be going *too* well?" I ask, pausing as I reach for my gym clothes. "I mean, it's happening fast, and he's wonderful and loving."

"When you know it's right, you just know," she says. "I don't think time has too much to do with it. You've been in love with him half of your life."

"True. And it's Ben. It's not like I just met him a month ago. I've known him forever."

"Exactly," she says. "Don't overthink it. Just enjoy it."

"Good advice," I reply and then hold the phone away from my ear as I pull my shirt over my head. "Lena will be here in a few minutes. She's going with me today."

"Cool. Have fun."

"Talk to you later." I end the call and throw a change of clothes into my gym bag, reach for my shoes and turn to the vanity to grab a hair tie, and then I simply freeze.

"What the fuck?" I take a deep breath and stare at the brand new bottle of Chanel No. 5 sitting on my vanity. I certainly didn't put it there. In fact, this morning the new bottle I bought of my favorite perfume was sitting in that exact spot. "Oh my God."

"Van?" Lena calls from downstairs. "I don't want to startle you! Your door was unlocked so I just came in!"

"In my bedroom!" I call back, my eyes still pinned to the bottle. Lena walks in, looking all cute and sporty in her workout attire.

"What's up?" she says and then frowns. "Your eyes are glassy and I'm getting a spooked out vibe from you."

"More than spooked," I reply, feeling sweat form on my upper lip. "Look."

She follows my finger to the perfume and frowns. "Okay."

"I don't wear that," I reply. "Ever. Lance made me wear it every fucking day of our marriage and I *hate* it. I didn't put it there."

Lena frowns and then closes her eyes and takes a deep breath. "I'm not as strong psychically as Mallory, but I don't feel an evil or malicious presence here, Van. Maybe your cleaning lady found it and put it there?"

I frown and shake my head. "Well, she was here today, but I threw it all out as I unpacked the boxes after the move. I don't know where she could have found it."

"Maybe you missed one?"

I exhale loudly and shrug. "Who knows? I guess it's possible." I reach for the bottle and carry it downstairs, throwing it in the garbage. "I'll ask her when she's back next week."

Lena smiles. "Good idea."

We leave for the gym and I set the perfume out of my mind, not wanting to give it any more attention today. If I let myself, I'll overthink it and work myself up into a frenzy, convinced that Lance is trying to mess with me from prison, and that just isn't possible.

I'm sure Lena's right. The housekeeper found it and set it out. It's certainly more expensive and fancier than what I normally wear, so she probably thought she was doing a good thing by displaying it. I'll just let her know that I don't want her to rearrange my things anymore.

"Someone had a good weekend," Lena says with a smile.

"Are you reading me?"

"Honey, I don't have to be psychic to feel the sex vibes rolling off of you."

I feel my cheeks pinken. "There might have been some sex."

"Uh huh." She parks in front of Ben's dojo and cuts the engine. "Good for you."

"Oh yeah," I reply, nodding. "It's good for me."

Lena snorts as she climbs out of the car and joins me as we walk inside. Some of the girls who take the class are already here, stretching on the floor of the classroom. Ethan, Ben's manager, is at the counter, talking to a muscular guy that I haven't seen before.

I glance around, looking for Ben, but I don't see him.

"I wonder where Ben is," I murmur.

"He's in there," Lena says, pointing to a smaller classroom. Ben's in there, instructing a woman.

And his hands are on her. She's a bit taller than me, and definitely younger. Blonde, with boobs that she definitely paid for.

And she's smiling up at my boyfriend like he hung the fucking moon. Ben's hands are on her hips and he's talking to her. She laughs like he's just said the funniest thing *ever* and braces her hand on his chest.

"Take a breath," Lena says. "This is his job."

"I'm okay," I lie and walk into our classroom.

I'm so *not* okay. I'm jealous as fuck and even though it's stupid, I can't help it. His hands are on another woman and she's freaking *flirting* with him. I'm not even in the same category as okay.

I'm pissed as hell, and the fact that this is his job doesn't make me feel any better.

Thankfully, class starts right away. This is the best place to let go of some pent up aggression. We spend the next hour punching, kicking, and sparring and when we're done, I'm dripping in sweat.

"I'm glad I wasn't your sparring partner," Lena says as we get ready to leave. "You kicked her ass."

"She's fine," I reply.

"Do you feel any better?"

"No." I glance around to see if Ben's around, and he's just saying goodbye to the hooker he was teaching while I was in class. "I know I said that I'd catch a ride home with Ben, but would you mind dropping me off?"

"Not at all," Lena replies. "Let's go."

"Van." Ben calls out to me, but I act like I don't hear him and don't turn around. Instead, I hurry to Lena's car and jump in. Ben walks out after us, and our eyes lock for a moment, but Lena takes off before he can open my door.

"He looks pissed," Lena says.

"I don't care. *I'm* pissed. And I also don't care that it's stupid to be pissed because this is his job and blah blah blah. Fuck that. His hands were all over that woman, and *I don't like it.*"

"I can tell," Lena says. "And frankly, I don't blame you. I wouldn't like it either."

"See? Good. I haven't been jealous in *years*. I can't even remember the last time, but all I can see is green right now. I want to punch that chick in the throat."

"Hey, he's your man and she touched him. That's a perfectly normal response."

"You're a good friend," I reply as she pulls into my driveway. "I can see why Mallory loves you so much, and I'm glad that you're part of our little circle now."

"Thanks." She smiles and waves as I walk to the front door. She waits for me to get inside safely before she drives away.

I have too much energy. I pick up my mail and thumb through the envelopes, but I don't really see any of it and I toss it all on the coffee table in my living room and then decide that although I just had an amazing workout, I'm not done.

I want to run.

And those who know me well know that running is *not* my thing.

But I don't know how to get rid of this energy without breaking stuff. So I take off down my street. I know which streets to stick to, and which areas are a bit shady. I'm not in good enough running shape to go far anyway.

Am I being stupid? I mean, she was a client. And the fact that she was flirting with him isn't really Ben's fault. *And*, he wasn't touching her inappropriately. My instructor touches me the same way all the damn time. But the difference is, she's a woman and not some dude that I would like to climb like an oak tree.

I circle around the corner of my block and run smack dab into a hard chest. Ben's arms wrap around me so I don't fall, and I immediately step out of his hold.

"What's going on, Van?"

"I went for a run," I reply and keep running back to my house, just three doors down. I don't look back, but I can hear him jogging behind me. He's not even breathing hard when we get to my front door, and I'll admit that the black T-shirt he's wearing does amazing things to his arms.

Those tattoos get me every damn time.

But right now, I'm pissed.

"Talk to me." Ben follows me inside and gently closes the door behind us. He's cool as the proverbial cucumber and I'm ready to come out of my skin.

"I didn't say there was anything to talk about."

"Stop it." My eyes whip up to his, and although he's calm, his eyes are annoyed.

*Good.* We can be annoyed together.

"Please tell me why you're mad at me."

"I don't know if *mad* is a good word for it," I reply and wander back to the kitchen to grab a bottle of water from the fridge.

"What word would you use?"

"Pissed. Irritated. Irate." I shrug and twist the cap off, chugging the water.

"Why?"

I shrug a shoulder, and that's about all Ben can take of me. He crossed his arms over his chest and leans against the wall, watching me.

"We can do this all night," he says.

"No, we can't because I'm asking you to leave."

Pain moves through his eyes now, and I feel like a grade A shit.

"I'm not leaving."

I cock a brow. "Fine. Stay. I'll leave."

"Enough." He grips my shoulders tightly in his hands and holds me in front of him. "What the fuck is going on, Savannah?"

"That woman had her hands on you!" I jerk out of his hold but I stay where I am and confront him. "And you had your hands on her. And it fucking pissed me off."

"The client?"

"If *the client* is a cute little twenty-something blonde with big tits, then yes. The client."

"Van—"

"I know!" I begin to pace now, just as frustrated with me as he is. "I know that it's your job and that there are clients and you have to touch them, but damn it, Ben, it was a cute girl who looked at you like you were dessert and she was going to eat you with a fucking spoon."

"Savannah." His eyes aren't hurt or irritated anymore. They also aren't full of humor, which is good for him because if he decided to make fun of me right now, I'd throat punch him.

"I didn't like it."

"I can see that."

"And I hate that I'm suddenly this stupid jealous woman—"

"You're not stupid."

"But I can't help it. You're *mine*, damn it."

The next thing I know, my back is pressed against the wall and Ben is kissing me like it's going out of style. His hands fist in my hair, his thigh presses against my core, and *I* want to climb him like a fucking oak tree.

His lips kiss down to my neck as he boosts me up, cradling his hard, denim-covered cock against me. My legs wrap around his waist.

We're both still fully clothed, but holy Hannah the sexiness is off the damn charts.

"She doesn't do this to me," Ben says, pressing hard against me. "No one does this to me but *you*."

"Damn right."

His eyes darken and he carries me to the guest room down the hall. There's no time to go upstairs. He sets me down long enough to strip us both out of our clothes and then throws me on the bed.

I don't even have time to be worried about the fact that I'm sweaty and probably smelly. He covers me and pins my hands above my head. His mouth and free hand are *everywhere*. My nipples are puckered and

223

my hips are moving in circles, desperate for him to fill me.

"Ben."

"That's right," he says. He grabs my chin. "Open your eyes. *You* are everything I want. I don't give a fuck about any other woman, client or not. Let them flirt and make a fool of themselves. It doesn't matter, Savannah, because *you* are all I think about.

"*You* are all I see."

I try to move my hands so I can touch him, grip his cock, and guide him inside me, but he holds me firm.

"I want to touch you."

"Not this time," he informs me. "I'm about one second away from being far rougher than I should be with you."

I frown. "I'm not fragile."

He swallows hard and I can see that he's struggling to keep himself in check.

"I'm safe with you," I say and kiss his bicep. "I *want* to touch you."

He releases my hands and his inhibitions all at once. He palms my ass in one hand, tilting my hips so he can easily slide inside me, and that metal rubs the length of me, making me groan.

"God I love that piercing."

"I love *you*," he growls and sets a fast, hard pace. "This is mine. *You* are mine, Savannah. Do you understand me?"

"Yes."

He's not being careful the way he has every time before. He's marking his territory, and it's the best thing I've ever felt in my life.

"Don't you ever fucking forget what you are to me," he says. His blue eyes are on fire and on mine.

"What am I?" I ask and watch in fascination as his eyes darken. His jaw tightens. His grip on my ass digs in just enough to sting.

It's fucking delicious.

"You're *everything.*" He kisses me, his lips much gentler than the rest of him. "You are the beginning and the end of me, Savannah. I don't work without you."

"You're *my* everything too," I reply. Suddenly, he pulls out and flips me over, slaps my ass, and slides inside me again. His legs are straddling mine, pinning me to the bed.

It feels *so good.*

So damn good.

"Shit, Ben, I'm gonna—"

"Fuck yes," he growls next to my ear. "Let go, love."

I couldn't hold back if I tried. I explode beneath him, my entire being shattering into a billion tiny pieces.

As I come down from the orgasm high, Ben kisses my shoulders and down my spine as he pulls out of me and helps me turn onto my back.

"Is that settled?" he asks.

"Oh yeah." I'm still working on catching my breath.

"Yeah, I think that's settled. But I think that once in a while you can remind me. Because that might have been the sexiest thirty minutes of my life."

"It might have been fifteen minutes."

"Whatever." I can't move yet, but I summon enough strength to cup Ben's cheek and smile up at him. "You're sexy."

"You're a challenge."

"I think I'm supposed to be a challenge."

"Well, then you're the world champion at it."

He grins and drags his knuckles down my cheek. "No more jealousy, Angel. There's no need for it."

"Are you going to keep teaching her?"

"Would you rather I didn't?"

"If I said that I'd rather you didn't, would you fire her?"

He chuckles, but he's safe now because I don't have the energy to throat punch him.

"I would pass her on to someone else, yes."

I stare up at him and think about everything that's happened. Not just today, but over the past few weeks, and I know without a doubt that Ben doesn't care about her.

"Just ask her to not touch you," I reply. "Unless she tries to punch you, I'd really rather she keeps her hands to herself."

He smiles and kisses my cheek. "I'll pass her on to Ethan."

"I trust you."

"That was never in question," he replies, perfectly calm again. "But she makes you uncomfortable, and there's no need for that."

"Thank you."

"All you have to do is say something when you're uncomfortable. I'll make sure to fix it. And not just when it comes to my job."

"Okay." I nod. "I'll remember that."

"See that you do."

# CHAPTER 15

"*D*oes it seem like this is happening fast?" I ask Violet during our counseling session the next morning. "I mean, we haven't *talked* about moving in together, at least not formally, but I'm starting to think about it, and it doesn't scare me."

"Savannah, you've known Ben most of your life. You didn't have to go through the initial getting to know each other stages. You've done that already. So, to admit that you love each other and want to move forward in your relationship is a logical next step."

"Right." I nod and rub my hands on my pants nervously. "But it makes me nervous."

"I can see that. Why do you think that is?"

"Because I worked hard to be independent," I reply, not even realizing that I felt that way until this moment. "And I'm afraid that if we live together, I might lose a piece of myself again."

"Well, that's logical too," Violet replies and nods thoughtfully. "I can see where you're coming from. But, something you're going to have to keep reminding yourself is that Ben is *not* Lance. They're completely different men, and the relationship that you share is different too."

"Boy, that's the understatement of the year," I reply. "Which brings me to something else to talk about."

"Okay, shoot."

I shift in my seat, gathering my thoughts. "My marriage was horrible."

"And now you hold the record for understatement of the year," Violet replies.

"I know." I grab my bottle of water and take a long sip. "It was the worst time of my life, and I truly believe that no matter what the future holds, it will never be as bad as it was while I was married to him."

Violet just nods, urging me to continue. I begin to peel the label off of the water bottle and focus on that while I continue to talk.

"While I lived it, I knew it wasn't right. That not every marriage was that horrible. But at the same time, I couldn't let myself analyze it. Because if I did, I really think that I would have had a nervous breakdown." I glance up to see her reaction, but she just arches an eyebrow, waiting for me to continue. "But now that I've been with Ben for a while, and I am in a healthy, loving relationship, I can finally see just how horrible it was before."

My eyes find hers again and I can't help the tears that come. "It was worse than anyone should have to go through. He didn't treat me like a human being, not to mention his partner in life. He treated me like I was a possession."

I bite my lip for a moment, wipe my eyes, and keep talking, unable to keep the words at bay.

"He's a horrible man, V."

"Yes. He is."

"And now I have something so beautiful with Ben, and I can't help but feel sorry for the woman I was before, because she was missing out on so much joy."

"Oh, Savannah."

My gaze whips up to hers and I'm mortified to see Violet crying. "You've never cried in my office before."

"I know."

"And even though you knew in your heart long ago that Lance was a horrible husband, you couldn't admit it aloud. Even to me."

I nod and wipe more tears from my cheeks.

"I'm so happy for you, Van. What you've found with Ben, and the healing that's happened in you because of that relationship is remarkable."

"Thank you." I sniff, relieved that the crying jag seems to have subsided. "Do you think I'm completely over it?"

"Well, that's a question only you can answer." Violet wipes her own eyes. "You've absolutely come a very long way, and you're much stronger now than you were when you walked in here two years ago."

"I am." I nod. "And I know that there will always be scars, and there may be moments that something triggers a knee jerk reaction. I can't help it when that happens."

"It should happen less and less as time passes."

I nod again. "I can see that. I'd like to keep coming to see you for a while."

"I don't think we're done quite yet," she agrees. "But, we could probably schedule appointments twice a month rather than once a week."

"Awesome." I stand and Violet pulls me in for a hug. "Thank you."

"It's been my absolute pleasure," she replies. "Are you off to work now?"

"I'm going to swing by my place to grab some things and then I'm headed to the office."

"Well, have a great day."

As I leave Violet's office and head toward my house, it feels like a weight has been lifted. A weight that I've carried around with me for a long, long time. It's amazing.

I pull into my driveway, surprised to see Ben's loaner car there.

"Ben?" I call out as I walk into the house.

"In the kitchen," he calls back. He's on the phone and he doesn't look happy in the least. "There are only three of us who take that home each night," he says.

He's rummaging through drawers, shuffling papers, and then hurries out of the kitchen and up the stairs to the bedroom. I sit in a stool at the island, waiting for him to come back.

"What's going on?" I ask as he walks into the kitchen.

"Ethan says the flash drive that we keep all of our financials on is missing." He pushes his fingers through his hair and exhales loudly. "Depending on who closes that night, it would be him, Shelly, or me that takes it home at the end of the night."

"You keep it on a flash drive? Isn't that a bit primitive?"

"The point is," he says, ignoring me, "that the passwords to bank accounts, balances, *everything* is on there. And my checking account was wiped out this morning."

"Oh my God."

"I keep the payroll and savings on my computer at home, so those are safe, but whoever did this took quite a lot. I have calls out to my bank and CPA, but it's a fucking mess."

"How can I help?"

He kisses my forehead. "Be patient with me today."

"I can do that."

He nods and fetches his car keys. "I'm going to check my place again, and then back to the office to tear the place apart. Do you need anything from me?"

"I think you have plenty on your plate," I reply. "I'm

good. I'll text you when I'm on my way home from work later."

He nods and waves as he leaves. Who could have stolen his financial information? I wander upstairs and change my clothes, then pause in the living room, glancing about in case I see something. Not that I know what the flash drive looks like, but it doesn't hurt to check.

The small pile of mail from yesterday catches my eye on the coffee table. I forgot to go through it.

I sit on the sofa and thumb through a utility bill, some junk mail, and a large, padded envelope. I tear it open and break out in a cold sweat. I'm numb.

What the actual fuck am I looking at?

Photos. Of me. Of Ben. At our jobs, coming out of the dojo, at dinner.

In my bed.

The photos fall out of my fingers and scatter over the floor. There's nothing else in the envelope. No note.

Just these photos.

*Oh my God.*

There's a knock at the door. I don't feel my legs as I stand to answer it, and can't even process quite who I'm looking at when the door swings open. The sun is blinding me. I shield my eyes.

"Lance?"

"We do look a lot alike, don't we?" He grins and walks in, pushing me backwards.

"Larry?"

"Oh good," he says, glancing down at the photos on the floor. "You got the package."

"What the hell is going on?"

"Jesus, Savannah, you're slow, but you're not fucking stupid. What do *you* think is going on?"

"Who took those photos?"

He smiles, but there's no light in his eyes. *Jesus, he looks just like Lance.*

My phone is in my pocket, but my fingers are shaking too much to be able to dial it.

"Don't do anything you'll regret," he says calmly. He picks up a photo of Ben and me sleeping in my bed and smirks. "Don't you look cozy in this one?"

"Why are you doing this?"

"Well, we're going to explain everything. Don't worry, we won't keep you in the dark. But first you and I need to go somewhere."

"No." I shake my head and back up. "I'm not going anywhere with you."

"Yes. You are."

"You don't know me very well if you think I'm getting in a car with you."

"I'll break your fucking arm, and then put you in the car and take you anyway. If you think I'm bluffing, you're more stupid than I thought."

*My God, he looks just like Lance.* No, he's not bluffing. Everything in me is screaming to *not* get in that car, but I don't see where I have a choice.

"Take your handbag and keys. We're not uncivi-lized," he says and smiles sweetly now. "We're just taking a little field trip."

He takes me by the arm and leads me out of my house, down the porch steps, and to my car.

"You're driving."

"I don't know where we're going."

He rolls his eyes and shoves me into the passenger seat, takes my keys, and starts my car. "Fine. I'll drive. But I hate driving."

"I hate being here with you, but it looks like we're both stuck anyway."

He arches a brow and pulls away from my house. "No wonder Lance smacked you around. You have quite the smart mouth on you."

I don't answer him. I turn my head and stare out the window and he drives in silence. The city slips away and we're out in the country for what feels like forever. We drive through Baton Rouge, and keep going until he turns off the freeway, following signs for the Louisiana State Penitentiary.

My head whips around. "You're taking me to the *prison?*"

He doesn't answer. He just smiles and shows an armed guard our identification. They don't even bat an eye as they let us drive through. We're led inside and to a small, windowless room with a table and three chairs set up for us.

"This is where inmates meet with their lawyers."

"Lance's lawyer isn't here."

"Yes, he is," Larry replies proudly. "He's assigned me as council now that his trial is over."

I can't breathe. I'm covered in sweat. I can't stop shaking. I have to look weak and vulnerable, which is *not* how I want to look to them, but I can't stop.

"They wouldn't normally let you in with me, but I made it worth someone's while to let me do pretty much whatever I want."

"You're paying them off?"

He laughs now. "Oh, Savannah. You're so naïve. If it wasn't so pathetic, it would be cute."

A door opens, and Lance walks in. The guard uncuffs him and he sits opposite me at the table, staring at me.

Staring *through* me.

"Well hello, wife."

"I'm not your wife."

He scoffs. "A technicality. You're still mine, Van. You'll always be mine."

I shake my head and stand.

"I want to leave."

"Sit down," Lance says in that calm, menacing voice he used every day of our marriage. I hesitate, but then obey. "Good girl."

"What do you want?"

"Show her," Lance says, never looking away from me as his brother opens a briefcase that I didn't even see him carrying. He pulls out hundreds of photos and spreads them over the table.

*Fuck.*

I can't swallow. I can't breathe.

"Look at how big young Sam has grown," Lance says, pointing at a photo of my sister's son walking home from the bus stop. "And how sweet Eli's baby and wife look in their backyard."

I sit still, numbly watching as he and Larry comb through the photos of every member of my family, all at different times of day.

Then Larry pulls out photos of Ben and me and Lance's smile slips.

"And now you're whoring yourself out to Ben?"

I don't answer, but rather sit in horror as more photos are pulled out. Ben and me, all over town. In our homes. With my family and his mom.

"You have someone watching us?"

"Clearly," Lance says and rolls his eyes like I'm stupid. "We see everything."

Larry tosses a photo of the Chanel No. 5 on my vanity onto the pile.

"You stopped wearing your perfume," Lance says.

"I hate that perfume."

"I don't give a fuck," he replies. "You'll fucking wear it. Every goddamn day."

"I'm not married to you," I remind him again. "I can do what I want. I can wear what I want."

"Okay." Lance sits back and crosses his arms over

his chest. "Let's talk about that. Larry, show her the last of them."

Ben throwing up at the side of the road. Ben getting beat up in front of his building. Ben and me standing on his front porch with the door open. Ben and me standing by his Jeep, right after the accident.

"I admit, the whole cut brake line thing was a bit dramatic." He shrugs. "But I kind of liked trying something out of the movies."

"All of this is *your* fault?"

"Oh, this and more." He grins again, looking so fucking smug. I want to kick him in the balls. "Is Ben having some financial trouble this morning?"

"What the hell, Lance? You're doing all of this because I'm not with you anymore?"

"Who do you think you are?" Lance asks, ignoring my question. "You're nothing, Van. You're a piece of shit. You're fat, you're horrible in bed. Jesus, fucking you is like fucking a dead fish."

It's all things I've heard before.

"Do you seriously think you deserve to be happy?" he continues. "You don't deserve *anything* except for the beating I gave you when you *thought* about leaving me."

"And you deserved the one Ben gave you in return."

Every tiny ounce of humor leaves Lance's face.

"You have two choices." He leans in now, pinning me in his stare. "You can break up with this prick, go back to living the way *I* say you may, and I'll leave Ben and the rest of your fucked up family alone."

"Or?"

"Or, you can keep seeing Ben. Fucking him. You can keep your hair short, and wearing your disgusting perfume, and pretending like I never existed in your world."

"I'll take that option."

"If you do, I'll—"

"You'll what? You'll be pissed and keep following me? Do you think I can't call the cops and my lawyer and put a stop to this?"

He tilts his head to the side, watching me. "No. I'll slowly destroy everyone you love."

"You can't do that."

His lips twitch. "I've already started. But let me be clear. I won't *kill* Ben. That's too easy. No, I'll make Ben's life hell. I'll destroy him. Financially, emotionally. It will be a constant battle, and he'll never know where I'll come from next."

"You talk a big game, Lance, but I don't believe you'll pull it off."

"We've been in your house," Larry reminds me. "And his. When you're sleeping. When you're fucking. We're always watching."

"And then I'll start with your family. This is going to be quite fun, actually, so I'm kind of hoping you go with this option. Look at how innocent and *safe* Sam looks while he walks home from the bus?"

"Keep your fucking hands off of my family."

He ignores me, and keeps looking through the photos. He holds up one of Mallory locking up her shop after dark. "Mallory shouldn't close her place up by herself after dark in the Quarter. Anything could happen. Oh, and look at this one! Your mama outside in her garden. She has earbuds in her ears. I'm quite sure she wouldn't hear someone come up behind her."

I'm seeing red. "You're threatening *my family.*"

"Oh, you know this isn't a threat, sugar. This is what's going to happen. You may have put me in here, but you didn't keep me from doing what I do best."

"Terrorism?"

"I'm just being a good husband. I'm helping you make good choices."

"You're crazy."

"Call me that again and you'll see how fast I can come across this table and choke you out. There are no windows in here."

*Oh my God.*

"If you're thinking of going to your brothers about this," Larry says, "you might want to think again. Because at any given moment, we have people watching them. In fact," he opens his phone and turns it around so I can see, "I just received this photo a minute ago."

It's of Ben coming out of his house.

"We bought the house across the street," he continues. "I have a sniper upstairs, and at any moment he could take Ben out."

He's winning. I'm never going to be free of him.

"You care about all of these idiots. I have no idea why," Lance says, as if he's talking to a good friend, joking around with him. "But you do. So my hunch is, you're going to ditch Ben and mind your manners from here on out."

"Is it because Ben beat the shit out of you?" I ask softly. "Because he's *better* than you?"

"He's not better than me. You chose me over him long ago. No, it's only partly because of the physical pain you allowed him to inflict on me. It's mostly because you're *mine*. And you don't get to be with anyone else. Ever. I won't allow it."

"You don't have a say."

He busts up laughing and points to the photos. "Have you heard anything I've said? Have I ever bluffed where you're concerned?"

No. No, he hasn't. Lance doesn't bluff.

"So, those are the choices. You remember your place and go back to behaving the way you should, or you continue this nonsense and I terrorize your family. Either way, I get what I want, so I'm really content with whatever you decide. See? I *have* changed. I'm willing to compromise."

There's a knock on the door and Larry immediately scoops up the photos and puts them back in the brief case.

"Take that home," Lance says. "It's okay, I have copies. Think about it tonight. I'll know what you decide in the morning."

"How?"

"Well, it wouldn't be fun if I shared all my secrets now, would it?" He winks and Larry passes my keys back to me. "You can drive yourself home now."

"Please don't do this."

"God, you're so fucking pathetic. So boring. You should go now, before I decide to have Larry follow you out and give you a black eye." He smiles and wiggles his fingers. "Bye, wife."

Bile rises into the back of my throat as I hurry out of the prison and back to my car. I throw the case in the backseat and get away as fast as I can. I have to call my brothers. Ben. Mama.

I have to call the police!

But Lance's face is still in my head, and I know in my heart of hearts that I've lost. He wasn't bluffing. He'll hurt them. He'll hurt them *forever.*

And I can't have that.

I turn on the windshield wipers and then frown when the water doesn't clear away.

It's not rain.

It's tears.

And a hole inside me so deep and wide that nothing will ever fill it up ever again.

## CHAPTER 16

~BEN~

"*I* don't know how this happened," Shelly says, in tears. I'm back at the dojo now, and Shelly, Ethan, and I are in my office, wracking our brains. "I *know* it was in my purse last night. I always zip it into the pocket inside."

"And you didn't drop your bag?" I ask. "Maybe you didn't zip it and it fell and the drive fell out?"

"No."

"Okay, look," Ethan says, holding his hands up. "It's missing. The bank is working on the fraudulent charges. There's nothing else to be done about it right now."

"You're right," I reply and squeeze the back of my neck. "It'll get sorted out. I'm going to hire someone to revamp our books so it's more secure. I should have done it a long time ago. This is on me."

243

"Shelly, you should call it a day," Ethan says. "You don't have any more classes today anyway."

"Thanks." She stands, but doesn't leave the room. "I'm truly sorry."

"Go regroup and we'll see you tomorrow," I reply and sigh when she closes the door behind her. "What a shit show."

"You can say that again," Ethan says. "But I mean it. We'll get it figured out."

"I know." Ethan leaves as well, and I reach for my phone to call Van. It rings and then goes to voice mail. "Hey, Angel. You're probably swamped at work. I just wanted to hear your voice. Have a good afternoon, and I'll see you later tonight."

I end the call and frown. Something has felt *off* for the past couple of weeks. There's nothing that I can see, it's just been a lot of shitty things happening, one right after the other.

I shrug and chalk it up to bad luck just as my phone rings.

"This is Ben."

"Hi, Ben, this is Sally." Her voice is shaking, putting me instantly on high alert. "Your mom and I are at the hospital."

"Why?"

"Well, I'd really rather tell you in person. We're in room 3344 at Tulane."

"I'll be right there." I end the call and rush out of my

office, filling Ethan in as I grab my keys and hurry out to the loaner car.

I fucking hate this loaner. It feels like it takes me an hour to get to the hospital, park, and get up to Mom's room. Sally's at her bedside and a doctor is talking to them both.

Mom looks like she's barely able to stay awake.

"Oh good, Ben's here," Sally says to the doctor. "This is Millie's son, Ben."

The doctor shakes my hand. "I'm Dr. Coltrain. We've admitted your mother, and I have to be honest, Ben, she's in bad shape."

"What's happening?"

"I haven't told him what's going on," Sally says. She's wringing her hands in nervousness.

"Your mother was given a lethal dose of Ativan."

"How?"

"Her prescriptions were delivered today, like they always are," Sally says, "and I gave her her meds, but there must have been a mix up at the pharmacy."

"Sally called an ambulance as soon as your mother started showing signs of poisoning," Dr. Coltrain says. "And we were able to counteract the medicine, but she's still a very sick woman."

She's sleeping now, as pale as the white sheets she's lying on.

"I expect her to make a full recovery, but she'll be with us for a few days. Today is going to be the worst of it."

"I can stay with her," Sally says, but I shake my head no.

"I'll stay. You go on home. I'd appreciate it if you can come up tomorrow."

"Of course." She stands and pats my shoulder. "I'm so sorry."

"Not your fault," I reply. When she's gone, I turn to the doctor. "What medicine did she take again?"

"We sent the pills to the pharmacy to be identified to be sure, but based on her symptoms, I think it was a very high dose of Ativan."

"That's a downer."

He nods.

"Was it enough to kill her?"

"Maybe," he says with a grim nod. "But we pumped her stomach and she's actually already looking much better than she did when she first arrived."

"Shit, she looks horrible."

"Hear you," she whispers without opening her eyes. I grin and kiss her forehead.

"You look beautiful."

She doesn't answer and the doctor closes his laptop. "I'll be here for another six hours. I'll bring the doctor who will take over for me tonight in to meet you before I leave. If you need anything, don't hesitate to push that red button."

I nod and sit quietly after the doctor leaves. When Mom is deep in sleep, I reach for my phone and dial Van's number again. This time it doesn't even ring, it just goes straight to voice mail, so I hang up and call her office.

"Savannah Boudreaux's office," Becky says in greeting.

"Hi, Becky, this is Ben. Can you please put me through to Van? It's an emergency."

"I'm sorry, Ben, she isn't in the office today."

"Of course she is," I reply with a frown.

"No, she never showed up. I presume she's working from home today."

"Thanks." I end the call and shoot a text to Van.

*Becky says you're not in the office today. Everything okay? Please call.*

When I don't hear from her thirty minutes later, I call Beau.

"Hey," he says.

"Hi. I'm at the hospital with my mom. There was a mix up with her meds, and she's going to be here for a couple of days."

"Shit, I'm sorry," he says. "How can we help?"

"Well, I'm fine for now, but I can't reach Van. I saw her this morning, but Becky said that Van never came into work today, and I can't get her to answer the phone."

"She probably has it turned off," Beau says.

"Maybe, but I have a bad feeling. Can you check in on her?"

"Sure. Do you want me to come up to the hospital with you?"

"No. Mom's sleeping. They'll kick me out when visiting hours are over. But please check on Van and tell her to call me."

"Will do."

But two hours go by and I don't hear from her. Beau texted and said he spoke with her. She wasn't feeling well and was napping at home.

Rather than call her like a goddamn stalker, I leave her be and plan to check in on her after I talk to the night doctor and leave for the night.

"Hi, my boy," Mom says groggily.

"Hey, how are you feeling?"

"Never been so sleepy in all my days," she says. "You should go. I'm just going to sleep."

"I'm going to stay until I can talk to your doctor, and then I'll go."

"Okay."

She falls right back to sleep, and less than thirty minutes later the nurse and doctor arrive to talk about their plan for the night.

"I recommend you go home," the doctor says. "She's sleeping comfortably, and if anything changes we'll call you."

"Thank you." I stand, but then turn back. "Do we know how the mix up happened? She doesn't even take Ativan, so it's not like it was just a mistake in dosage."

"We don't know," he says with a frown. "But it's been reported and there will be an investigation."

I nod and leave, wanting nothing more than to see

Savannah, and see for myself that she's okay. Thankfully she doesn't live too far away.

Her car is in the driveway, and the lights are on in the living room.

"Hello?" I call out after I let myself in with the key she gave me and walk inside. Van comes out of the kitchen with a steaming mug of tea, sets it down, but doesn't sit. She also doesn't look me in the eyes.

"Are you okay, Angel?"

"Fine." She forces a smile and pulls her zip-up hoodie tightly around her. "Beau told me your mom isn't feeling well?"

I cock my head to the side, watching her. Something is *way* off. "She's going to be fine. What's going on with you?"

"Oh, nothing," she says. "Just a bug of some kind."

I step toward her, but she quickly backs away. "You shouldn't come near me. I'm sick."

"Someone once told me that if you're taking care of someone who's sick you can't get sick yourself."

"That's silly," she murmurs. "You know, Ben—" She doesn't finish the sentence. She takes a deep breath and clears her throat. "You know, I think things are moving kind of fast between us."

I narrow my eyes, watching her. She pushes her hair off of her face and bites her lip, but her eyes still won't meet mine.

"I mean, we've really rushed things, and I was talking to my counselor this morning, and she pointed out that maybe we should slow things down a bit."

"That's a lie," I reply calmly. She's upset about something, and she's trying to run away rather than let me help.

"It's not a lie," she snaps. "I'm not comfortable with how quickly our relationship is moving. I think it's a good idea to just take a break for a bit and catch our breath."

"I don't need to step back."

"Well, it's not all about you," she says. She's irritated and pacing the living room now.

"Why didn't you answer your phone earlier?"

"I was busy."

"You didn't call after you heard about Mom."

"You don't get to tell me when I have to call you," she says, working herself up. "You don't control me. I'll call you when I damn well want to. And if I want to stop seeing you, I'll do that too. It was never going to work." She laughs humorlessly. "How did we ever think it would work?"

"Because we're in love with each other and being without you is a hell I don't want to ever experience again?"

"Stop it with the pretty words," she yells. "You say all of the right things and then you have sex with me and make me feel things, and I give into you because it all feels good, even if that's not what I really want. It's not fair!"

"What do you want?"

"I want you to go. I want to stop seeing you because it's only going to end badly, and then it'll hurt everyone we love. I can't be selfish about this, Ben. I've told you that from the beginning."

"You're not being honest with me."

"Stop calling me a liar!" She's panting now.

"You're having a panic attack."

"Don't tell me what I'm having." She looks at me now, square in the eyes, and the pain there almost brings me to my knees.

"Let me fix this." My God, she's shattering me into a million pieces. "Savannah, I don't know what made you come to this conclusion today, but you're wrong. We *can* make this work."

"I don't want to do this," she whispers. "I can't do this."

"Savannah."

"You need to go."

"No. I'm not leaving you like this."

"Goddamn it, Ben, just go."

I move toward her, needing to pull her into my arms, but she flinches, putting her hand up as if to deflect a blow, and it stops me in my tracks.

"Did you just *flinch*?"

"Yes. I'm obviously afraid of you," she says.

"What the fuck, Savannah?"

"Don't you swear at me," she replies. "I want you out

of my house. I'll pack your things and you can get them off of the porch tomorrow afternoon."

I shake my head, staring at her, but she doesn't move. Her face doesn't change. She's panting, her hands in fists at her side, and she's waiting for me to leave.

So I do. I make myself turn away and walk out the door, down to my car, and drive away from her house.

What in the ever loving fuck just happened?

Once at home, I can't stop pacing. Thinking.

I'm so fucking *pissed off.* What is she thinking? I don't buy the whole *my counselor says* bullshit. What happened today?

I want to march back over there and make her listen to me, but that will only end in disaster. I won't sleep. I can't sit still.

So I call Ethan.

"I know it's late, but I need a favor," I say when he answers.

"What do you need?"

"I need you to meet me at the dojo. I need to kick someone's ass, and you are one of the few I know who can keep up with me."

"I could use a few rounds in the ring with you. It's been a minute since we sparred."

"I'm heading there now."

Aside from the Boudreauxes, Ethan is one of my closest friends, and one of the best Krav Maga masters

I've met. He's an asset to my team, and an excellent sparring partner.

He's already there when I arrive. It's dark inside, with just the small dojo lights on.

"What's up, man?" he asks as I walk in.

"I don't want to talk about it," I reply. "But you're going to need a helmet because I'm fucking pissed and I'm going to try to kick your ass."

He grins. "Fun." He's smart enough to get a helmet, and I advance, not pulling any punches. Ethan is shorter than me, but just as strong. He takes me down and we struggle for a few minutes until I work my way loose and reverse our positions. I punch him and then roll away, giving him a chance to get back up.

We go like this until both of us are lying on the mat in exhausted heaps, both of us on our backs.

"You're pretty worked up," Ethan says as he struggles to catch his breath. "Is it the financials?"

"That's only a piece of it," I reply and sit up. "It was maybe the shittiest day of my life."

"Shittier than that time you lost in the ring to that kid from Canada?"

"Yes."

"Shittier than the day you stopped fighting for the MMA?"

"Yes."

"Do you miss it?"

"The MMA?"

He nods.

253

"No. I beat my body up daily so I could whoop ass in a cage. I'm too old for that shit now. I like my business."

"You're good at it." He tugs his helmet off and winces. "It's a good thing I wasn't stubborn and told you to shove the helmet up your ass."

"I could go another round."

He glances at me, surprised. "I'm done, man. Go hit the bag. Or go home and fuck your girlfriend."

I growl and stalk away from him.

"Ah, she's one of the problems." He laughs. "Makes sense. My wife drives me batty eighty percent of the time. But she's the best thing I'll ever have in my life."

"I don't really want to talk about women," I reply. "You can take off. I'll punch the bag for a bit."

But after he leaves, I don't have the energy to keep punching the bag. I can't go home. There are too many memories of Van there, and I'll just make myself crazy.

So, I go to my office and lay down on the couch. It's quiet here at night. Haunted as fuck, with footsteps up in the attic. I use it for storage, and where the footsteps are, is currently covered in boxes.

But that doesn't bother me. I'm used to it.

What bothers me is that Savannah has shut me out. If she thinks it's over, she doesn't know me very well.

# CHAPTER 17

~SAVANNAH~

*S*eeing the pain on Ben's face when he left my house is conceivably the most horrible thing I've ever seen in my life. Every word I said to him cut me inside, and I wanted to run after him to tell him the truth, to beg him to help me.

But I couldn't.

I can't.

Ben can't fix this. *No one* can fix this.

Except me. I just pray that when it's all said and done, Ben can forgive me.

I turn out all of the lights on my way up to my bedroom. I don't expect to sleep tonight, so I grab a notebook and pen and settle on the bed, ready to make several lists.

. . .

*IT'S WARM TODAY. Almost too warm, especially out here on the water. I'm wearing a super wide brimmed hat, protecting my face and shoulders from the sunshine. Daddy and I are floating lazily on the lake, our fishing poles lying on the bottom of the boat.*

*"Fish aren't biting today," Daddy says. "But that's okay. Sometimes it's nice to just sit on the water and enjoy the quiet."*

*I nod and lean back, closing my eyes. "It's a nice day. A bit warm."*

*"You never did like the hot weather."*

*I grin. "I don't know how I could have been born in Louisiana and not like warm weather, but you're right. I actually prefer a cold, rainy day. But it's nice to be out here with you today."*

*And then I remember. Pain slices right through me, just as bright as the day he died.*

*"I've missed you," is all I can say. Daddy smiles softly and reaches out to pat my knee.*

*"I'm with you," he says. "You can't always see me, but I'm never too far away."*

*"I'm glad you come to me in dreams," I reply and sigh happily when the sun slips behind a cloud. "That's better."*

*"I love spending time with you, baby girl, but we have something to discuss."*

*"We do?"*

*There's no humor in his eyes now as he nods solemnly. "You know we do."*

*Lance. The prison. The photos. It all hits me again, and I just feel ashamed.*

*"I'm sorry," I whisper.*

*"What, exactly, are you sorry for?"*

*"I've put the family in danger again."*

*He shakes his head impatiently and takes his fishing hat off his head long enough to scratch his hair and then pushes it back on.*

*"For such a smart little thing, there are moments that I want to throttle you."*

*"You never throttled me," I reply. "And I'm not being dumb."*

*"Savannah Jean Boudreaux, you didn't do anything wrong. And you know it."*

*"It's happening again," I murmur. "He's threatening to hurt our family, all because I fell in love with Ben all over again and he and I are trying to be happy together. Lance will never sit back and let me move on from him."*

*"You know what to do," Daddy says gently. "You've already put the plan into motion. It's a shame that Ben was caught in the crossfire."*

*Thinking about it hurts. "I hurt him."*

*"Yes. You did."*

*"But he would try to fix this for me, and I don't need him to do that."*

*"No, you don't." He smiles now and the knot in my stomach loosens. "I'm so proud of you, Savannah. You don't look defeated like you did before. You look good and pissed off, and that's just how it should be."*

"I am *pissed*," I reply honestly. "That actually might be the biggest understatement ever. I'm so blinded by anger. He scared me, like he did before. Maybe worse this time because he showed me the pictures of the babies."

"He's playing mind games with you, Van."

"I know. It took me several hours to let the terror subside and realize that he's just trying to scare me and bend to his will. But I'm not his wife. And even if I were, no one *has* the right to treat me that way."

"There's my girl," he says with a smile. "You're an amazing woman, Savannah. Ben's a lucky man."

"If he forgives me," I reply and feel my eyes well with tears. "He might not."

"You haven't done or said anything unforgivable," Daddy replies and pats my knee again. "You'll work this out and be better for it."

"You've always had so much more confidence in me than I have in myself," I reply.

"Because I can see you, Daughter. I see you the way you should see yourself. And you're beginning to."

"I wish you hadn't gone away," I whisper. "Dreams aren't enough."

"We want it all, don't we?" He nods and adjusts his hat again. "I'm here. And your brothers love you. You're surrounded with people that you can lean on and ask for help when you need it."

"None of them are my daddy."

"True." He smiles. "It has been the pleasure of my life to be your father. Now, you go take care of your business."

*"Will I see you again?"*

*"I'll come visit now and again."* He picks up his pole. *"Let's get us some dinner."*

THE SUN IS ALREADY UP and shining in my bedroom when I waken. I didn't think I'd sleep at all, yet it seems that I slept for about nine hours, which is good because I'm going to need the rest.

It's going to be a busy day.

"GOOD MORNING," Declan says as he pulls his front door open. "You could have called to let me know you were on your way over. I would have made breakfast."

"Oh, I'm not hungry," I reply. *I can't call because my phone is tapped.* "Can I come in?"

"Of course." He backs up so I can come into the house and closes the door behind me. "Van's here!" he yells out to Callie.

"I hope I didn't wake you guys up."

"We didn't work last night," he replies as he leads me back to the kitchen where Callie is making a cup of coffee.

"Hi, Van," she says with a smile.

"Hey." I love Callie. She's perfect for my brother. But right now, I need to talk to just him. I glance over at Declan and he immediately knows.

"Hey, Cal, can you give us a few minutes?"

"Sure." She finishes pouring the cream in her coffee and kisses Declan as she walks out of the room. "I'll be upstairs."

"Thank you," Dec says, watching me closely. "What's going on?"

"Why do you think something's going on?" I ask, evading the question. "I could use a cup of coffee."

"In a minute. First, tell me what's on your mind."

I don't want to tell him. I probably shouldn't have come here, but I needed to see my twin brother. "Well, I broke it off with Ben."

He stares at me for several long seconds as if I just told him that I sold my share of the company. "Why?"

I shrug. It's killing me to lie, but I have to keep up the façade. If I don't, Larry could hurt someone.

"It was always a bad idea," I say at last. "It was best to end it before it made things really bad between our families."

"Bullshit," he says and crosses his arms over his chest. "Try again."

"I'm serious," I reply. "Not to mention, things were moving really fast. Too fast. We want different things."

"Still not buying it."

"Do or don't, it doesn't change it. Ben isn't the one for me."

I pull a piece of paper out of my handbag and pass it to him, holding my finger over my lips so he doesn't read it aloud.

*I have this under control. Trust me. Please don't interfere.*

His eyes whip up to meet mine and he cocks his head to the side, scowling. I shake my head, keeping him from speaking.

"So, I think I'm going to take a day or two off of work and get my shit together. If you need me, text me, okay?"

"Okay." He's searching my face, worry written all over him. "Are you okay?"

"I'm actually doing just fine. I'm going to be great."

That, at least, is true.

"Call me if you need me," he says, and I can hear what he's not saying. *Call me when you can tell me what the fuck is going on.*

"I will." I give him a brief hug and walk to the front door. "Tell Callie I said I'll see her soon."

And with that, I shut the door behind me. I need my family to know that something is up with me, but I can't tell them exactly what. Not yet. Not until I have this all figured out, and I know without a doubt that no one can hurt them. Declan is the one who can read me the best, and I can trust that he'll wait for me to reach out to him. The others would push me aside and try to slay my dragons for me.

I don't need that.

I toss my cell phone in my handbag, fully intending to ignore it for the next few days, and pull out a throw away phone that I bought this morning. I pull away from Dec's house and keep an eye on my rear view.

Someone is following me. They followed me here from my house. I don't know how much they can hear, or what they might have wire tapped, so I bought this disposable phone.

I dial the number that I haven't had to call in almost two years, but one I'll never forget.

"New Orleans Police Department, Lieutenant Jacobs' office."

"Hi, this is Savannah Boudreaux. I need to talk to Lieutenant Jacobs, please."

"Savannah, we haven't heard from you in a while," Lieutenant Jacobs' assistant says. "I'll put you right through."

"Thank you."

The line is silent and then he's on the line, his voice low and firm. "Savannah?"

"Hi. I need your help."

"How quickly can you be here?"

"I'm headed there now. I'll be there in ten minutes."

"I'll be waiting."

He ends the call and I take the long way to the precinct. I get on the freeway and speed up, weaving in and out of every lane to lose the tail. To my utter shock, it works, and I take the next exit, then double back to the police department. I park and hurry inside, straight to Lieutenant Jacobs' office.

"It's been a minute since I've seen you," he says as he

holds his door open for me. "No calls while I'm in this meeting."

"Of course," his assistant replies.

He closes the door behind us, and rather than sit behind his desk, he sits in the chair next to mine. He was always good at making me feel comfortable with him, and aside from my dad, there's no one else I'd trust more to help me. Lieutenant Jacobs has to be nearing sixty. He has salt and pepper hair and brown eyes that have seen more than their share of horrible things.

"What's going on?" he asks.

"A lot. You might want to record this."

His eyes narrow, but he reaches for his phone, opens the app, and sets in on the desk in front of me. "Okay, we're ready."

I nod, take a deep breath, and spend the next hour telling him everything that's happened over the past few weeks, beginning with Ben and I deciding to start seeing each other. I recount Ben being poisoned, the car accident, Ben getting beat up, and every other thing I can think of, including the *accidental* mix up in Ben's mom's medication.

Then I show him all of the photos.

He doesn't say anything until I'm done with the story.

"Larry took you, against your will, to the prison?"

"Yes."

He nods and then sits back and looks over at me with hard brown eyes.

Cop eyes.

"That mother fucker." I blink rapidly, surprised. "I knew we should have had a restraining order against Larry as well."

"That's on me," I reply. "I truly believed he was different. I didn't realize that he and Lance were in cahoots."

He blows out a gusty breath and asks me to go through it all again. It's an exhausting afternoon.

"Can you help me?" I ask.

"Darlin', not only will I help you, but we're going to make sure that they can never try to hurt you ever again. I thought we accomplished that before, but we didn't wrap it up tight enough. You have my sincere apology for that."

"He's evil," I reply with a shrug. "No normal person would ever dream that he'd come up with half of what he's done. Am I going to have to go back there? Wear a wire, or something?"

The thought of that alone makes me break out into a sweat.

"No." He smiles kindly. "I would like for you to spend the next forty-eight hours doing what you're doing. Play along while I get my team in place to take them down. There will be no mistakes made, no reason for a lawyer to come back with a hole in our investigation. These men are all going away for the rest of their lives. Can you do that?"

I cringe, but nod. "I'm hurting my family by lying to them, but I didn't see another way. He threatened them, and I know him. He would follow through. So I thought that if it looks like I'm playing along, he wouldn't hurt anyone before I could come to you."

"That's absolutely the best thing you could have done," he replies. "I'm going to get working on this right now. I don't want to call your cell phone if I have news."

"I bought a disposable." I rattle off the number for him.

"You're a smart woman."

"I've learned a lot in the past two years," I reply with a sad grin. "I can protect myself."

"Good. I'll call you the second we have them in custody."

I nod and stand to leave, then turn and give him a hug. "Thank you."

"You're going to be just fine."

I nod and walk out, confident that Lieutenant Jacobs will take care of Larry, Lance, and whomever they've hired to help them take my family apart.

He made a big mistake in thinking that I'd roll over and take his shit.

~

"NO ONE CAN REACH you on your cell phone," Beau says the next afternoon as he walks into my office. "I've received calls from Mom, Gabby, and Mallory today. Actually Mallory called three times."

I do my best to keep my face neutral, hating myself for lying. "I must have forgot it at home. Sorry they're bugging you."

"Also, you're acting weird."

I frown and look around my office. "I'm working. How is that acting weird?"

"I don't know." He leans against my desk and taps his lips with his forefinger. "But when you ignore Mal, I get to hear about it. She thinks something's up."

"Well, this is one time that she's wrong."

"She's wrong once in a while," he concedes and then hurries to say, "but don't tell her I said that."

"Your secret is safe with me."

*I seem to be keeping a lot of secrets lately.*

"Seriously, is everything okay? I heard about Ben."

"I'm surprised you didn't bully your way into my office to grill me about that."

"I rarely bully," he says. "And I thought you might need a little space."

"You're right. I guess I've been processing a lot the past few days. That's probably why I forgot my phone this morning. If you get any more calls, just tell them that I'll call them back later."

"Mama wants you to come over for dinner tonight."

I sigh and push my fingers through my hair. That's a no-go. I can't lie to my mama.

"Do you mind telling her that I just don't feel up to it?"

"Is there anything else I can do for you?" he asks sarcastically, making me smile. "Change the oil in your car? Order in take out? Pick up your dry cleaning?"

"Yes to all of that," I reply with a sweet smile. "Thanks for being awesome."

"Now you're trying to soften me up for something," he replies.

"You always assume the worst."

"Of course I do," he says. "I run a business."

"*We* run a business."

"Well, you help sometimes, but mostly we gave you this big office to make you feel important."

I laugh now, a full out belly laugh and it feels fantastic. "Oh good, I can just stop reading all of these boring reports and instead have them all sent to you."

"On second thought," he says, "maybe you do work more than a little bit."

"Maybe I do," I agree. "I needed that laugh."

"I know." His face sobers now. "If you think that you're fooling anyone, you're wrong. We love you, and we can see that something isn't right."

"Beau—"

"Let me finish. When you decide to let us in, we're here. All of us."

"I know. But really, I'm fine."

"You're better than *fine*, Savannah. You're the most amazing person I've ever met."

I simply sit back and stare at my brother in utter shock. "I won't tell Mallory that either."

"She knows," he replies with a smile. "And she gets it. You are pretty great, and that's why we all start to worry when it looks like something might be wrong. Because of all the people in the world, you deserve a break."

"Beau, I love you. And I have everything under control."

*That, at least, isn't a lie.*

"Okay then, that's all I needed to know."

He kisses the top of my head and then walks out of my office, closing the door behind him.

*Please call me, Lieutenant Jacobs. I need this shit show to end.*

# CHAPTER 18

~SAVANNAH~

*D*ay two of the hostage situation, as I've come to think of it, was more exhausting than day one. I shouldn't have gone in to work, and if it weren't for the fact that I have to make things look as *normal* as possible, I wouldn't have. It's not like I'm getting much done. I stared at the same report for two days straight and never turned the page.

I finally left the office an hour early today and took a drive around the city. Driving calms me. I like to listen to music, or turn the radio off altogether and enjoy the silence.

Also, I'm ninety-eight percent sure that my car isn't bugged, so I can relax a bit.

I've just turned down my street, toward my house, when the throw-away phone rings.

"Yes," I say.

"It's done," Lieutenant Jacobs says on the other line.

He's the only one with this number, so there's no question of who it is. "Larry is in custody, as are the two men they hired to survey you and your family."

"We're safe."

"You are. I have more to tell you, but I have a ton of paperwork to get through here, three men to interrogate, and I need to go have a meeting at the prison."

"Thank you. Thank you so much."

"You're welcome. Go live your life, Savannah."

He ends the call as I pull into my driveway, right next to Eli's car.

I frown and then shrug. It's not unusual for Eli to drop in, although it's not as common now that he has a wife and a baby.

I walk into the house and freeze at the scene before me.

Eli is sitting on the couch, and every single photo that Lance gave me is spread out before him on the coffee table. I laid them out last night, as a reminder to myself of why I had to be strong and trust that Lieutenant Jacobs would take care of things in the right way.

But I certainly didn't intend for my brother to see them.

"Hello," he finally says. I turn to close the door, but instead find Declan, Beau, and Ben walking up my steps. I whirl around to look at Eli and he just nods. "Yeah, I called them."

"Great," I mutter and walk into the room. I haven't

figured out how to explain this yet. I was taking it one minute at a time.

And now I have four angry men in my living room. Ben won't even look me in the face, but he's looking at the photos. They all are.

"Savannah," Declan says, his voice full of pain as he looks over at me.

"How long?" Eli asks before I can say a word. "How long has this been going on?"

"First, I need to tell you that it's over," I reply and stand firmly, my hands on my hips. "As of about five minutes ago when Lieutenant Jacobs called me."

"So you *do* answer your phone," Beau mutters and holds the photo of Mallory closing her shop after dark.

"It was a throw-away phone. My cell was tapped."

"What the fuck is going on, Savannah?" Eli demands, his voice deceptively quiet.

"Don't you dare swear at me," I reply. "Put the photos down. They don't matter anymore."

They do as I ask, and then they all just stare at me, except Ben, who still hasn't said a word and won't look at me.

I've lost him.

"It seems Lance didn't take kindly to me moving on with someone else," I begin. It takes me a while to tell the whole story again, as I don't want to leave anything out. When I finish telling them about the call I received this afternoon, the room is quiet.

"You didn't have to do this alone," Declan says.

"You *shouldn't* have done this alone," Eli agrees. "Van, why did you keep this from us?"

"Because you would have tried to fix it."

"Of course we would have," Beau says. "That's what family does, Van."

"No." I shake my head and sigh in frustration. "I spent the majority of my adult life living in fear because I thought I was protecting you. All of you. And damn it, I was protecting you now, but not out of fear. Not this time.

"I didn't need you to fix this for me. *I* fixed it. I knew what to do. He scared me at first, I'm not going to lie. But nothing I did after I left the prison was out of fear. It was strategic, and it kept us all safe while the police did their jobs."

"Jesus," Beau whispers and pinches the bridge of his nose. "I want to throttle you and hug you, all at once."

"Daddy said the same thing," I reply and smile when they all look at me in shock. "I dream of him sometimes. He said that to me the other night."

I swallow hard and then look them all in the eyes. Especially Ben. "I'm sorry for the worry and now the fear that I caused you. I love you all so much. I know that you feel like you need to protect me, and I wouldn't have you any other way.

"But I'm a strong person. Stronger now than I ever was before, and I need you to trust in me. I need you to know that I would never do anything to betray you, or hurt you. And damn it, if there's a threat against my family, I'll do whatever it takes to protect them.

"He threatened to hurt you. To hurt the babies." I let a tear fall. "I can't have that, and I'll be fucking damned if that evil piece of shit is ever going to think he can do that to me again. He underestimated me, and he lost."

"You're incredible," Declan says and takes my hand in his, giving it a squeeze. "I also want to throttle you, but I get it. We all get it."

Eli and Beau nod, and Ben has walked to the window. His hands are in his pockets, and he's staring outside. He hasn't said a word.

"I'm going to have to go through another trial, and it's going to suck, but that's okay."

"And for that, we'll be with you," Eli insists and pulls me in for a strong hug. "No more lies, Van."

"No more lies," I agree. "I'm not good at it anyway."

After a few more hugs, my brothers leave. Ben's still at the window and silence screams around us.

I sit in a chair and wait, watching his muscles twitch under his black T-shirt. Finally, he turns around and locks his eyes onto mine.

"I'm so fucking pissed off," he says. His voice is steel, matching every tight muscle in his body.

"I'm sorry."

"No," he says, shaking his head. "I mean, yes, I'm not happy with you, and we're going to talk about that, but this rage is directed at *him*. All over again."

"I took care of it," I insist.

273

"He sat in a room with you and showed you all of the ways he wanted to destroy you and your family," he says, making me swallow hard. I hadn't thought of it like that. "He sent out people to terrorize you."

"And you," I reply. I shuffle through the photos until I find the one of the sniper. "He bought the house across from yours and had a man there with a rifle ready to kill you. Ben, *he's* the reason you got sick, and your brakes were cut. He made it clear that the longer I stayed with you, the more he would make sure you suffered."

"Being *away* from you was more suffering than he ever could have inflicted on me," he says, stunning me. "You let him come between *us.*"

"Only until they were arrested," I insist. "But if I've screwed this up so badly that you're done, I understand."

"I feel...*betrayed*," he says and lets his hands fall to his sides. "You did this on your own, and I thought we were partners. You didn't let me save you."

"Ben." I finally walk to him and cup his face. "You already saved me. It was time I saved *myself.*"

He crushes me to him, his strong arms locked around me. His face is buried in my neck, and it feels like he'll never let me go.

"Don't ever let me go," I whisper.

"God, Angel, you destroyed me."

"I'm so sorry," I reply and kiss his cheek, his chin. "I had to play along, or else he would have done something horrible. And if anything were to happen to you, Ben, I don't think I'd survive it."

"Baby." He kisses me now, long and sweet, as if he's relearning every inch of my mouth.

I catch a whiff of the perfume that Lance insisted that I wear, and it makes me sick to my stomach.

"Ben?"

"Yes, baby."

"I have to take a shower. I've been wearing *his* perfume, and every time I smell it, it makes me sick. I need to purge this house."

"Let's do it." He takes my hand and leads me to the kitchen and fetches a plastic bag. "Lead the way."

I pull him behind me, up the stairs and to the bedroom. The first thing I do is throw the Chanel No. 5 in the bag, then walk into my closet and purge the last of the clothing he bought for me years ago. It's expensive, and it seemed wasteful to throw it away before, but I don't even blink an eye as I shove every blouse and dress into the bag.

The last thing I reach for is my wedding band and engagement ring. They're in their respective boxes, tucked in the back of a drawer. I don't even open them, I just toss them in the bag.

"You're throwing those out?"

"To be honest, I think it should be donated to a women's shelter."

His lips twitch. "That's a great idea. I'll sell the jewelry too and donate that money as well."

"Ben, you don't have to do that."

"Yeah, I do. Let me do this." He ties the bag closed. "I'll be right back."

I stay where I am and hear the front door open and then several minutes later he's climbing the stairs again.

"It's all out of here."

"That feels good."

He nods and leads me into the bathroom. Rather than start the shower, he runs a bath. "I'd like to sit with you in the bath."

"No complaints here," I reply.

He strips us both naked, and we sink into the hot water, not wanting to let go of each other. He begins massaging my feet and I reach for the soap and a sponge, washing the last of the perfume off my neck and wrists.

When I'm done, I sit back and sigh. "I was so afraid that I'd lost you for good."

"Same here," he says quietly.

"I said some pretty horrible things." My eyes find his. "I'm so sorry. I didn't mean them, and it was killing me, but I had to make it look real."

"It *was* real."

I nod slowly. "Yeah. And it was hell."

"I'm not a controlling man, Savannah, but I *am* a man. I love you with everything in me, and I will always want to protect you. I don't know any other way to be."

"I don't want you to be any other way. This will *never* happen again."

"No. It won't." He pulls me to him. I straddle him and lay against his chest. "You're everything good in my life, and you're *mine*. I protect what's mine."

"So do I." I lift my head and smile at him. "So do I, Ben. And that's what I was doing."

"I know." He kisses me softly and then takes the kiss deeper, stronger. I rise up on my knees and then sink down over his hard erection, and we both moan in relief.

"Missed this," I mutter against his lips. He can't respond. He grips my hips and guides me up and down in the most delicious pace, until we're both a panting, orgasmic mess.

I collapse on top of him and kiss his chest, impressed that I can move any part of me.

"Angel?"

"Yes."

"I'm going to wash your hair."

*He can still smell it.*

"Okay. Do I have to move?"

He chuckles. "Yes." He guides me back to the opposite side of the tub and then steps out of the water. Without drying off, he urges me to lean forward and begins to wash my hair. I close my eyes and sit still, letting him scrub the soap into foam, and then rinse the soap out. His hands are big and strong, and it feels good to let him take care of me.

When he's done, he lifts me out of the water and wraps me in a towel, then leads me to the vanity in my bedroom.

"Have a seat," he says.

The excitement from the last few days has caught up with me. I'm exhausted, both physically and mentally and he knows.

He combs my hair out, then blows it dry. I sit and watch him through half-closed eyes and admire the way his muscles flex with each motion.

"You're just ridiculously handsome," I murmur when he flips the dryer off.

"I won't be leaving," he says.

"No, I definitely want you to stay with me tonight."

"Ever," he replies after we both get into the bed. It's early, but it feels like I just ran a marathon.

"Ever?"

"Ever." He kisses my lips and snuggles his naked body against mine.

"Does this mean you want to live in my house?"

"Do you prefer it here?" he asks, and I can see that if I say yes, he won't hesitate.

"Home is where you are," I reply sleepily. "Here or there, it doesn't really matter."

"I love you, Savannah," he whispers in my ear as I feel sleep pulling me under.

~

"ARE YOU SURE ABOUT THIS?" Lieutenant Jacobs asks me three days later. I've asked him to meet me, Ben, and the rest of my family at the prison today. It's a gloriously beautiful day outside, matching my mood.

"Oh, I'm sure."

He nods and leads me to a room. I go in alone, but there's an observation room connected to this one with a big, mirrored window. They can see in, but I can't see them.

But I know they're there.

Another door opens and in walks Lance. He's in handcuffs and ankle cuffs, and this time they don't let him loose.

I'm not that pompous.

I'm surprised to find that looking at him doesn't make my stomach tighten, or bile rise in the back of my throat. My heart doesn't race.

I feel disgust.

"What do you want?" Lance asks.

"A couple of things," I reply and lace my fingers on the table top. I don't move my eyes from his because I want to *see* him as I speak. "First, I want you to take one last long look at me, Lance, because this is the last time you'll ever see me."

"That's awfully optimistic of you," he says with a smirk, but I can see in his eyes that the confidence from a few weeks ago is gone.

"No, it's true." I sit for a moment and let him look at my face, my breasts, my hair. "Do you see me?"

"You're right in front of me."

"Oh, that doesn't matter. I was right in front of you for years, but you didn't see me. Do you see me now?"

His lips pucker but he doesn't reply.

"Good. Because you're looking at the woman who broke you, Lance." He smirks again, but I keep talking. "You tried to break me, but you didn't. *I* took *you* down, and I want you to sit in your tiny cell and think about that for the rest of your pathetic life."

"Fuck you."

"No. No, you won't ever do that again either." He moves to stand, but I cock an eyebrow. "Sit the fuck down."

He tilts his head to the side and drops back in his seat.

"I didn't say you could leave."

"What is this, Van? You show up here and act all tough? You're not tough. You're *nothing*. You're a pathetic piece of shit, and you may have got my brother arrested, but he's not the only contact I still have on the outside. I can have your family killed any time."

I don't turn around to see, but Lance's eyes rise above my head and I know the observation window has been turned off and that he can see all of my family sitting there, listening.

"Oh, I brought them along."

He glares at me, but it doesn't matter.

*He doesn't matter.*

"You can't hurt me, or them, ever again. It's over right now. I'm ending it."

He snarls. "You don't say when it's over." He's yelling now, and I stand, turn my back, and walk away. "Do you hear me? You don't say! I say!"

The door shuts behind me, finally closing that chapter of my life for good.

Ben meets me in the hall and pulls me in for a hug. "So proud of you, Angel."

"Me too," I reply and smile up at him, and the rest of my family standing behind him. "Let's go home now."

# CHAPTER 19

~BEN~

*hree months later.*

"It's such a pretty day," Van says as she tilts her head back and soaks in the sunshine. I have the top down on my new car as we drive to the Inn, the wind and sunshine on our faces.

Every time I look at her it's like a punch in the gut. Is it possible that she is more beautiful every day?

"Why are we going to the inn?" she asks.

"I thought we might have another picnic," I reply, only lying by omission. I think this is one lie that she'll easily forgive.

"Fun," she says happily. The past few months have been the best of my life. My mother has fully recovered from the medication fiasco, and is doing well with Sally's company. My business is healthy again.

And Van is by my side.

Life doesn't get much better than that.

I pull up to the inn and take Van's hand in mine. Rather than go up to the door to talk to Gabby, I immediately lead her around the house toward her tree.

"You're in a hurry," she says with a laugh. "Are you hungry?"

"Something like that."

"You've been acting weird all day. Are you feeling okay?"

*Aside from the ball of nerves in my stomach, I'm peachy.*

"I'm just hungry," I reply and kiss her hand. The sun has begun to set, setting the sky into a riot of color. We walk around a bend in the trail and Van stops in her tracks.

"Oh my," she breathes. "Not just a picnic after all."

"Maybe a fancy picnic," I reply. Gabby and Charly did an amazing job of setting up a table and chairs with a pretty cloth over it. There's a bouquet of flowers, and twinkle lights hanging from the branches of the tree overhead.

"It's something out of a fairytale," she says and begins to walk slowly toward it. "Did you come up with this?"

"I might have had some help," I admit. "But the place was my idea. I just thought you'd enjoy a pretty picnic in your favorite place."

"You thought right," she replies and sits when I hold her chair out for her. "This is really lovely."

I pour us each a glass of wine and take a long sip to

bolster my confidence. Not that I'm having any second thoughts.

I just want it to be perfect. She deserves nothing less.

She's staring up into the tree, at the lights and the lightning bugs floating overhead. I'd originally planned to wait until after we'd eaten for the big moment, but I don't think I can.

I need this.

So, I take Savannah's hand, kiss her knuckles, and completely toss the speech I'd prepared out the window.

I need to just speak from the heart.

"You're a special woman, Savannah Boudreaux. I've known that since we were young. I don't feel like the time we didn't have together was wasted because it made us both into who we are today, and without that, we might not be together now."

I swallow and keep going.

"That being said, the thought of spending even one day without you from now until my dying day is a torture I wouldn't wish on my worst enemy. I don't want to know a day that doesn't have you in it. You're the best part of every day."

I move out of my seat and kneel next to her and watch as her eyes fill with tears.

Please, God, let them be happy tears.

"So, I'm going to ask you, in this special place, to be

mine always. Marry me, Savannah. Spend your life with me."

"Oh, Ben," she says and watches as I slide the ring on her finger. Then she's in my arms, hugging me tightly. "Of course I'll marry you."

"Right now."

"What?" She pulls back and stares at me in surprise, then glances about and her jaw drops. Our family and friends have gathered around us, smiling.

"Why is she just sitting there?" Sam asks his mom, making me laugh.

"Yeah, are you just going to sit here?" I ask her.

"You want to get married *right now?*"

"Yes, ma'am."

"We don't have a marriage license."

"A technicality." I laugh when she scowls at me. "I want to have this moment with you, with the people closest to us, to make this promise to each other."

"Let's do it," she says and jumps up. "You've all been keeping this a secret?"

"He might have threatened us with violence if we told," Callie says with a grin. "Plus, this was a fun secret."

Charly, Gabby, and the rest of the girls come to stand at Van's side, while all of the men stand by mine. Our mothers are holding babies and grinning from ear to ear as they look on.

"I'll start," I say and clear my throat. "Savannah Boudreaux, I'm here to make you a promise. A solemn vow that I will be true to you, love you, protect and encourage you every day of my life. I will forsake all others—"

"Yeah, you will," she says.

"and never betray you. You will have my respect, and my heart, forever."

She takes a deep breath and smiles as she begins to speak.

"Benjamin Preston, I never thought this day would arrive. I dreamt of it, often, as a young woman and then as a grown woman. You are everything I've ever needed. I promise you, here in this special place, that I will love you, be true to you, protect and respect you all of the days of my life. I will probably not obey, but I will keep you on your toes."

Our family laughs, and she smiles up at me before she continues.

"I will forsake all others, and lift you up in love and encouragement. You will have my heart, forever."

I lean in and kiss her, softly at first, and then dip her back, earning applause.

I tip my forehead against hers. "Thank you," she says.

"This is entirely my pleasure, Angel."

## EPILOGUE

## ~BEAUREGARD BOUDREAUX~

*One year later.*
　　My lovely bride is sitting in the swing on the back porch of our home, rocking a baby slowly, watching our family in the backyard.

Children are playing. Couples are kissing and laughing.

My family is whole and happy. Healthy.

"Look at them," she whispers. "I feel you here."

I'm sitting next to her. I can feel the heat coming off of her and she lays her hand in her lap, her palm up.

So I take it in mine and wish with all my might that she could feel me.

"You're here," she says again. Her voice is soft, and sounds the way it did when she was eighteen years old, and I met her on a group date with a bunch of our friends. Seeing her was a punch in the gut, and I never left her side after that day.

Well, until *the day.*

"I'm here," I reply, even though she can't hear me.

"Look at our babies," she says with a smile. "All married, most of them having babies of their own."

She glances down at the infant sleeping in her arms. "This is our newest. Little Penelope. Goodness, I hope they don't call her Penny." She chuckles. "Although, I guess Penny isn't so bad. I am so happy for Ben and Savannah."

I brush my fingertips over the baby's head, and smile when her brow furrows. It's amazing how the little ones can sometimes see me.

"That man hurt our girl," she continues. "But sometimes family is more than blood. They've given this little one a wonderful home, and Van says they aren't done. She wants a whole house full of babies."

"I'm so proud of you," I tell her, the way I always do. "I know it's not easy without me. Lord knows, I wouldn't have held it together if you'd left ahead of me, darlin'."

"I miss you," she says, and then smiles softly. "I can feel you holding my hand."

I give it a squeeze. "I'm always here."

"You're with me, and I know that," she replies, making me smile. "You're watching over our babies."

"And you."

"And me."

Oh, how I love her. All of them. And I'll be here until she's ready to join me.

But there's plenty of time for that.

"Look!" Sam yells, catching her attention. "Ailish just threw the ball to Dad!"

She nods and smiles, careful not to wake the baby.

"They're such good people. Good work ethic, kind, happy. They're everything we ever wanted them to be, and more that I never dreamed of. You'd be so proud of them."

She pauses to watch and rock, holding my hand.

"You're here," she says again. It's a comfort to her, and I make sure to let her know I'm here as much as I can.

"I'm here." I smile and sit with the love of my life, watching over our home. Our children, and our children's children. "And I'm a patient man, my love. You take your time."

## NEWSLETTER SIGN UP

I hope you enjoyed reading this story as much as I enjoyed writing it! For upcoming book news, be sure to join my newsletter! I promise I will only send you news-filled mail, and none of the spam. You can sign up here:

https://mailchi.mp/kristenproby.com/ newsletter-sign-up

ALSO BY KRISTEN PROBY:

**Other Books by Kristen Proby**

**The With Me In Seattle Series**

Come Away With Me
Under The Mistletoe With Me
Fight With Me
Play With Me
Rock With Me
Safe With Me
Tied With Me
Breathe With Me
Forever With Me
Stay With Me
Indulge With Me
Love With Me
Dance With Me

Dream With Me
You Belong With Me
Imagine With Me
Shine With Me
Escape With Me

**Check out the full series here:** https://www.
kristenprobyauthor.com/with-me-in-seattle

**The Big Sky Universe**

**Love Under the Big Sky**
Loving Cara
Seducing Lauren
Falling for Jillian
Saving Grace

**The Big Sky**
Charming Hannah
Kissing Jenna
Waiting for Willa
Soaring With Fallon

**Big Sky Royal**
Enchanting Sebastian
Enticing Liam
Taunting Callum

**Heroes of Big Sky**

Honor

Courage

**Check out the full Big Sky universe here:** https://www.kristenprobyauthor.com/under-the-big-sky

**Bayou Magic**

Shadows

Spells

**Check out the full series here:** https://www.kristenprobyauthor.com/bayou-magic

**The Romancing Manhattan Series**

All the Way

All it Takes

After All

**Check out the full series here:** https://www.kristenprobyauthor.com/romancing-manhattan

**The Boudreaux Series**

Easy Love

Easy Charm

Easy Melody

Easy Kisses

Easy Magic

Easy Fortune

Easy Nights

**Check out the full series here:** https://www.
kristenprobyauthor.com/boudreaux

## The Fusion Series

Listen to Me

Close to You

Blush for Me

The Beauty of Us

Savor You

**Check out the full series here:** https://www.
kristenprobyauthor.com/fusion

## From 1001 Dark Nights

Easy With You

Easy For Keeps

No Reservations

Tempting Brooke

Wonder With Me

Shine With Me

## Kristen Proby's Crossover Collection

Soaring with Fallon, A Big Sky Novel

Wicked Force: A Wicked Horse Vegas/Big Sky Novella
By Sawyer Bennett

All Stars Fall: A Seaside Pictures/Big Sky Novella
By Rachel Van Dyken

Hold On: A Play On/Big Sky Novella
By Samantha Young

Worth Fighting For: A Warrior Fight Club/Big Sky
Novella
By Laura Kaye

Crazy Imperfect Love: A Dirty Dicks/Big Sky Novella
By K.L. Grayson

Nothing Without You: A Forever Yours/Big Sky
Novella
By Monica Murphy

**Check out the entire Crossover Collection here:**
https://www.kristenprobyauthor.com/kristen-proby-
crossover-collection

## ABOUT THE AUTHOR

Kristen Proby has published close to sixty titles, many of which have hit the USA Today, New York Times and Wall Street Journal Bestsellers lists. She continues to self publish, best known for her With Me In Seattle, Big Sky and Boudreaux series.

Kristen and her husband, John, make their home in her hometown of Whitefish, Montana with their two cats and French Bulldog named Rosie.

facebook.com/booksbykristenproby

instagram.com/kristenproby

bookbub.com/profile/kristen-proby

goodreads.com/kristenproby